"YOU'RE NO KILLER, JASON," VAL SAID QUIETLY.

"I could have killed you tonight."

"That was as much my fault as yours. Here I tell you not to get too close to the edge of the broken floorboards, and then I go and do it myself. My fall was an accident, and you know it."

"Accidents seem to happen when I'm around." He placed a hand over hers, moving her fingertips to his lips. "I don't want anything to happen to you."

It was already too late. Things had been happening since the day she'd walked into his house, feelings she couldn't control. Just the touch of his lips was like dynamite, sparking an explosion to the tips of her toes.

She melted against him, tilting her head so he found her mouth. His lips played over hers, the sensations a thousand times more exhilarating, the danger more real than a fall.

This was no monster holding her. This was a man, strong and caring. A man torn with doubts and burning with desire.

A man she could love. . . .

WHAT ARE *LOVESWEPT* ROMANCES?

They are stories of true romance and touching emotion. We believe those two very important ingredients are constants in our highly sensual and very believable stories in the LOVE-SWEPT line. Our goal is to give you, the reader, stories of consistently high quality that may sometimes make you laugh, sometimes make you cry, but are always fresh and creative and contain many delightful surprises within their pages.

Most romance fans read an enormous number of books. Those they truly love, they keep. Others may be traded with friends and soon forgotten. We hope that each LOVESWEPT romance will be a treasure—a "keeper." We will always try to publish

LOVE STORIES YOU'LL NEVER FORGET
BY AUTHORS YOU'LL ALWAYS REMEMBER

The Editors

Loveswept ®741

DARK TEMPTATION

MARIS SOULE

BANTAM BOOKS
NEW YORK · TORONTO · LONDON · SYDNEY · AUCKLAND

DARK TEMPTATION

A Bantam Book / May 1995

Bantam Books are published by Bantam Books, a division of Bantam Dou-
bleday Dell Publishing Group, Inc. Its trademark, consisting of the words
"Bantam Books" and the portrayal of a rooster, is Registered in U.S. Patent
and Trademark Office and in other countries. Marca Registrada. Bantam
Books, 1540 Broadway, New York, New York 10036.

PRINTED IN THE UNITED STATES OF AMERICA
OPM   0 9 8 7 6 5 4 3 2 1

My thanks to Dr. Michelle T. Valella,
Optometrist, and her staff for their
help with this book.

ONE

"Nowadays every town and city in the United States has a haunted house at Halloween time. If you want Slaterville's to bring people from miles around, it's going to have to be different. More spectacular, frightening, and mysterious than any other haunted house in Northern California."

Valerie Wiggins parked her white Ford in front of a run-down, peak-roofed mountain cabin and cursed herself for standing up and giving that speech at the last WIN meeting. The squeaking door didn't get oiled, it got volunteered. It was now *her* responsibility to create a different haunted house, *her* job to make sure it was more spectacular, frightening, and mysterious than any other haunted house around.

Just what she needed, another job.

She didn't have the time. She didn't have the energy.

Cut the bull, she told herself as she stared at the cabin. The truth was, she did have the time. And the energy. And she didn't mind being in charge of the project. What she didn't want to do was talk to the man who lived in this house.

"We have just the person who can help us turn our haunted house into a success," she'd said at the meeting that night. *"Living right outside of town."*

As if every woman in the room didn't know about Jason McLain.

So now, thanks to her big mouth, she was the one appointed to talk to Slaterville's newest and most infamous resident. His reputation alone scared most of the other women.

His reputation scared Val.

Unless you knew, you'd never guess a man who'd won three Academy Awards for special effects lived in this house. If he was as rich as the papers had said, he sure wasn't using his money to upgrade his property. In the six months since he'd moved to Slaterville, he'd done nothing to improve the exterior of the old Dalton place. The fence was broken in several places; beneath the snow, the small patch of lawn that had existed years before was no more than weeds; the bushes around the house were overgrown and dying; and the porch sagged. It and everything needed a fresh coat of paint.

The only changes she could see from when the place had stood abandoned for years, and now, were that the broken windows had been replaced and heavy drapes and venetian blinds kept passersby from looking inside. There were certainly no signs of life. The snow hadn't been shoveled from the walkway, no smoke curled from the chimney, and no lights showed behind the closed drapes and blinds. There was nothing to indicate anyone lived in the cabin except the tire tracks that led to the garage near the side door.

Or perhaps away from it.

Almost hoping he wouldn't be home, Val opened her car door.

Jason heard two raps at the side door and grumbled into the near darkness of his living room. It had to be Bud, back from the store. He'd said he was going for a six-pack of beer, but he'd probably bought more and couldn't open the door.

Again there were two raps.

Light.

Hesitant.

Jason pushed himself up from the sofa and started toward the kitchen. Why had Bud come anyway? he wondered. It wasn't as though an invitation had been issued. The past was better forgotten, and that included friendships. Besides, in the past three years, Bud hadn't exactly been Mr. Stand-By-Your-Side.

Jason had to admit, if only to himself, that that had hurt.

He shook his head as he walked between the sink and the table, both of which were piled with dishes. Dammit all, he'd left Hollywood to find solitude, to get away from the memories. Two and a half years of being harassed by the police and media had been enough. His own doubts were enough.

If Bud expected him to be Mr. Jovial, he'd driven five hundred miles for nothing, and a few beers wouldn't change that.

Val shivered as she stared at the closed door. The breeze sweeping down from the mountains was icy, but she doubted that was the reason for her shaking legs. The last time she'd been this nervous had been just before she took her state boards.

Should she knock again? she wondered, the muscles in her stomach twisting into a tighter knot.

Maybe another time would be better. Earlier in the day, when the sun wasn't about to set, when the sound of the wind whistling through the trees wasn't so spooky, and when every shadow didn't seem so eerie.

Maybe next month.

Maybe never.

She was about to leave, a sense of relief pouring over her, when she heard footsteps inside. Turning back toward the door, she waited, the knot once again tightening in her stomach. The pounding of her heart drowned out all other sounds, and an urge to run and hide warred with her sense of mission.

Then the door opened, and he was there.

She'd seen his face—the piercing dark brown eyes, the unruly brown hair, the unsmiling mouth—on the front pages of so many newspapers and tabloids, and on so many television newscasts, it was almost familiar to her. Nevertheless, she'd never realized he was so big, so tall and broad shouldered. His size made her want to shrink back. His scowl froze her where she stood.

"Who in the—" he started, then stopped. She sensed he recognized her, though she wasn't sure how. They'd never met. The only times she'd ever seen him in person were when he'd driven by her place, and then he'd never looked her way. Since she was now bundled in a heavy wool coat, a scarf around her neck, mittens covering her hands, and slacks and boots protecting her legs and feet, there wasn't much of her exposed to recognize.

"Mr. McLain," she began, trying to remember what she'd been going to say. The icy wind blew against her back, sending another shiver down her spine. She knew he had to feel it straight through his cable-knit sweater and jeans. "May I come in?"

"Why?" he asked, a guarded look in his eyes and a scowl on his face.

"Because it's cold out here." And because she was afraid that at any moment he was going to slam the door in her face, or she was going to turn and run.

He didn't move. Glaring into her eyes, he challenged her to look away, and it took every ounce of her assertiveness training to keep her gaze locked with his.

Seconds felt like hours, and her nerve was rapidly waning. Finally he stepped back and gave the slightest of nods, and she sucked in a bracing breath and forced her reluctant legs to take her into his kitchen.

He closed the door behind her, and she pulled off her mittens, stuffing them into her coat pockets. The kitchen was shadowy, light barely filtering through the closed venetian blinds. The atmosphere of the whole house was dark and intimidating, just like the man. Even the dirty dishes, glassware, and cups piled on the kitchen table seemed to form ominous shapes.

"Okay, what do you want?" Jason asked, not moving from the door.

To get the hell out of here! her mind screamed.

Ignoring the fear spiraling through her, she managed to find her voice. "My name's Valerie Wiggins . . . Dr. Valerie Wiggins. I'm the optometrist in town."

"And what? You make house calls?" His scowl deepened, his eyes narrowing. The chiseled lines of his face created a sense of granite, and the only softness she could see in him was a sprinkling of gray streaking the brown of his hair.

"No," she said hesitantly, then silently swore at herself. In the myriad possible scenarios she'd mentally practiced for, she'd been in control. Been decisive. Been relaxed.

She certainly wasn't relaxed now.

But then, this was for real. She was actually talking to Jason McLain, expert in special effects, three-time Oscar winner—and possible murderer.

Forgetting her prepared spiel, she tried to explain her purpose. "I'm also one of your neighbors. I live about a half mile down the road."

"I know," he said bluntly.

He knew.

That meant he *had* recognized her, and those times he'd driven by when she was outside working in her yard, shoveling the walk or feeding the birds, he *had* noticed her.

Just as she'd noticed him.

Noticed that he drove a blue Jeep Cherokee, didn't exceed the speed limit, often wore a brown leather bomber jacket and battered brown hat—like Indiana Jones—and always kept his gaze straight ahead. Or so she'd thought.

He'd noticed her.

Again a shiver ran down her spine, but this time not from the cold. Not liking the exhilaration she felt, she hurried to state her mission. "I'm here on behalf of WIN. That's W-I-N. The acronym stands for Women

In Need. We're a nonprofit organization made up of volunteers. We need your help."

"I don't usually give donations," he said, but reached into his pocket.

"No," she said quickly. "I mean, we always welcome donations, but that's not why I'm here. What I need is your expertise."

"Expertise?" His dark brows lifted suspiciously.

"On a haunted house. It's our annual money-making project, and in the past it's really helped us meet our budget. But now, it seems, every town and community in the Sierras is doing something like this at Halloween time."

"So?"

"So if we want people to come to ours, it needs to be different. Special."

Jason was beginning to understand. "*Special* meaning special effects?"

"Yes."

"You want me to help you with special effects for your haunted house," he repeated.

"Yes." She smiled, hesitantly and hopefully, and he felt his guard slip.

For some reason, from the very first day he'd moved to Slaterville, he'd noticed Dr. Valerie Wiggins. Not that he'd known until a few minutes ago that she was a doctor, nor did he understand why he was fascinated by her. He wasn't getting involved with a woman. Never again.

It was too dangerous for others.

She wasn't what he'd call beautiful or stunning, certainly not by Hollywood standards. In fact, if he had to describe her in one word, he'd say wholesome. Yes, she had a wholesome look about her.

She was about average height, maybe five feet five or six, and her best features were her short, curly brown hair and her big china-blue eyes. And, perhaps, her mouth. He hadn't really noticed before, but she did have a nice mouth—full and lush.

He looked away from her face. The bulky blue coat and tan slacks she was wearing didn't show off her figure, certainly not like the stirrup pants and silk blouse he'd seen her in a few months ago, but even then he wouldn't have called her *Playboy* material.

Yes, "wholesome" was the word to describe her.

She was the kind of woman every mother wanted her son to bring home.

Not that his mother wanted him bringing anyone home.

And not that any woman would go with him.

As direct, even bold, as her gaze might be, Jason knew Valerie Wiggins was no different. She might be smiling now, but she was afraid of him. Her uneven breathing gave her away, as well as her guarded stance. She was ready to run for the door at a moment's notice, and that irritated him.

He was tired of being viewed as a monster, of people avoiding direct eye contact and whispering behind his back. Maybe this woman didn't look down or away, but the same question was going through her mind that was in everyone's mind.

Did he kill his wife?

Upset with himself for even hesitating, he growled out his answer. "I'm through doing special effects.

You're going to have to find someone else." He reached toward the doorknob. "It was nice meeting you."

"Please," she said, her voice soft, not whiny. "All I need are some ideas."

His hand poised on the doorknob, he obliged. "Okay. Here's an idea. Rig up a ghost on a pulley. Now go."

She shook her head. "We already have a ghost on a pulley. I was thinking more in terms of moving figures —animated models. That is what you do best, isn't it?"

"Was," he said firmly. "Past tense." He was through with that part of his life, through with anything and everything that reminded him of the past.

"You could tell me—us—how to create them. What would work the best, what we would need."

It was obvious she wasn't going to leave, at least not willingly. Why was it people had decided to invade his house today? First Bud. Now Dr. Valerie Wiggins. He didn't want either around. They threatened to make him think . . . to make him feel.

With a grumble he walked toward her. "I don't have the time."

As he neared she tilted her chin up so she was looking directly into his eyes. He had the disconcerting feeling that she could see far more than he wanted revealed. Simply being in the same room with her was unnerving. She might be wholesome looking, not really his type, but dammit all, he found her attractive.

"When will you have time?" she asked.

"Never!" He turned away and walked out of the kitchen into his living room. "I assume you can let yourself out."

Val could, but she wasn't ready to leave. Nothing

had been settled, and she knew she'd never find the nerve to come back. Persistently she followed him. "All I'm asking for is a *little* of your time. For a few ideas."

"Well, I'm out of ideas," he snapped, and spun around.

He stopped and faced her so quickly, she walked straight into him. Body collided against body, soft against solid, her breasts flattening beneath her coat and sweater. Large hands touched her arms, balancing and steadying her, making her feel small and vulnerable.

His fingers gripped her coat sleeves, and she sucked in a breath. She should be afraid, but fear wasn't the emotion ricocheting through her body. Stunned, she stared up at him.

Her eyes, she was sure, reflected the same shock that she saw in his, the same awareness. Something was happening, feelings that shouldn't be there—tingling sensations playing over her skin, a shiver of excitement mixing with the heat of anticipation. Even through the layers of their clothing, she could feel the rapid beat of his heart. Her own pulse was racing as wildly, rushing the blood to her head, leaving her dizzy.

Words needed to be spoken, but none came—not from her, not from him. All she could do was stare into eyes as dark as the night and wonder why she hadn't noticed how thick his lashes were.

Her reactions were confusing her. She wasn't looking for romance. She didn't want to feel anything, not with this man.

Not with a man who might be a murderer.

For months she'd read and heard his claims of innocence, and all the while the media crucified him. Every piece of dirt the reporters could find made it into print or onto the six o'clock news. A jealous row with his wife years before her death became front-page headlines. The death of his brother and his estrangement from his parents was fodder for lunchtime gossip. The media tried, convicted, and hanged him. It was the jury of his peers that hadn't been convinced.

An acquittal on the grounds of insufficient evidence, however, wasn't the same as a verdict of "not guilty." Everything those newscasters and journalists had suggested could be true. And here she was in his house—in his arms.

It scared and excited her.

How long they might have stood there staring at each other she would never know. Before either of them said a word, the side door flew open and a male voice announced, "I'm back!"

Jason reacted first, releasing his hold on her arms and moving away. "Bud," he murmured, as much to himself as to her.

She turned and looked into the kitchen. Standing where she had been only a minute before was a lean, thirtyish-looking man with unruly blond hair, a boyish smile, and a six-pack of beer in each hand. "Well, well, well," he said, grinning and giving her a quick up-and-down scan before glancing at Jason. "Sorry. If I had known you were entertaining, I would have knocked."

"I wasn't entertaining," Jason said firmly. "This is a neighbor. The local eye doctor. Dr. Valerie Wiggins, meet Bud Henke."

"Just call me Val," she said, hoping her cheeks weren't as flushed as they felt.

"Bud's one of the top special effects men in the business," Jason continued. "Ask him for some ideas for your haunted house."

"Haunted house?" Bud repeated as he walked over to the refrigerator.

Jason filled him in. "She's looking for a gimmick to draw bigger crowds. She wants more money for some charity."

"For a safe house," Val explained. "We operate a safe house for abused women." She glanced back at Jason. The moment they'd shared was gone, and he was now eagerly pawning her off on someone else. It shouldn't bother her, she barely knew the man, yet for some reason it did bother her.

"How big of a budget do you have?" Bud asked, the fizz of a beer being opened coinciding with the refrigerator door closing.

She faced him again. "I'm sure we could come up with a few hundred dollars."

His laughter was immediate, and he looked at Jason. "You want to tell her the kind of budget we usually work with?"

Afraid she could guess, she tried to make their resources sound better. "I'm also sure I could get some of the merchants in the community to donate materials."

"Right." Bud walked toward her, his gaze once again sliding over her body, this time slower, more assessing. "Who up here in this ghost town is going to have miniature hydraulics engines to donate?"

"I don't know," she admitted. She did know, however, that she didn't like Bud Henke's sarcasm and roving eyes *or* Jason McLain's scowls and gruffness. "Do we need miniature hydraulics engines?"

"For what you want, you need them," Jason said.

"Well then, can either of you think of anything else? Something that would bring more people to our haunted house, yet not cost an arm and a leg? Our problem is we need just about every cent we have for our safe house. That home is important to a lot of women. It's the only one for miles around, and though people may think abuse doesn't happen in small communities, it does."

"Maybe what you need is a different money-making project," Bud suggested.

Maybe, but they had to make do with what they had. She shook her head. "The house was given to us years ago. It's here, and people know about it. All we need is to make more people want to come."

" 'Build it and they will come,' " Bud said.

"All I'm asking for are ideas." Desperately she looked at both men.

Bud took a swig from his beer. Jason sighed. "What if I promise to think about it?"

She heard the unspoken remainder of his question. Will you leave? he was asking. She wanted more. "Would you really think about it?"

"I would."

She didn't know what else to say, short of begging.

"Hey," Bud said, wiping his mouth with the back of his hand. "If I were going to be up here longer than just tonight, I'd see what I could come up with." He glanced at Jason and grinned. "Of course, considering that little scene I walked in on, maybe you'd like me to find a motel room for the night."

Little scene? Val groaned silently. What could she say to explain? That she'd followed Jason into his house and ended up in his arms? And what was worse, that she'd gotten all fuzzy headed and emotional about it? Here she was a thirty-year-old woman, yet simply bumping into a man had started her thinking like a teenager. It wasn't until Bud had arrived and Jason had stepped back and released her that any sensibility had returned.

"You don't need to find a motel," Jason muttered. "Dr. Wiggins is leaving."

He glanced at her, and she nodded. Evidently a promise that Jason McLain would think about ways they could make the haunted house special was all she was going to get. For her to stay any longer, in a house that was growing darker by the minute, with two men she didn't know, was not a wise move.

Well, she amended, she didn't know Bud. With Jason, she knew too much; too much about the day his wife opened their wall safe and a gun went off in her face. He'd been at the studio that day, and the police had found no fingerprints to link him to the gun, but he was an expert in special effects. Rigging a gun to go off on cue was basic know-how in his line of work.

No matter what the media said, or the jury, only one person knew if Jason McLain was innocent or guilty.

She wasn't that person.

Bud walked with her to the side door and held it open for her. Jason stayed where he was in his shadowy living room, an ominous, dark figure, his expression unreadable.

"I've seen just about every movie you've worked on," she called back to him. "Everything seemed so real. It was wonderful. I'm sure you'll think of some ways to make our haunted house succeed."

He half smiled.

"My office is right on Main Street, between the hardware and the barber shop. I'm usually there eight to five Wednesdays and Fridays and nine to noon every other Saturday. Give me a call or stop by and we can discuss this further."

Discuss it in a more neutral and safer setting, she might have added. Somewhere where she wouldn't end up in his arms. A place where common sense ruled her actions, not emotions.

All she got from Jason was a nod.

"Well . . ." There seemed to be nothing more to say. "Thank you."

TWO

"Thank you," Val repeated to herself once she was back in her car.

What an idiot she was. She'd thanked him for scowling at her, growling, frowning, and being downright hostile. For throwing her a crumb.

"*I'll think about it.*" That was all he'd said. Nothing more.

She was definitely an idiot. He'd touched her, and she'd gone all weak-kneed and gooey-eyed. She knew what his promise meant.

He wouldn't think about it.

"So, are you going to do it?" Bud asked as he turned on the kitchen light.

"Do what?" Jason mumbled, squinting at the glare. Like it or not, it looked as though Bud was spending the night.

"You know what. Are you going to help her?"

"I told you earlier, I'm through with special effects."

"I know what you said earlier, but that was before I found you with a woman in your arms. A man can change his mind."

"I'm not changing my mind." What he needed to change was the subject. "I suppose you expect me to feed you dinner?"

"Why do you think I came?"

"Good question."

Bud grinned. "Just happened to be in the neighborhood?"

"Now why don't I buy that?"

"Well, I do have to stop by ILM tomorrow."

That made more sense, Jason thought, but Marin County and George Lucas's Industrial Light and Magic Company were still a long way from Slaterville. He walked over to his refrigerator, but before he opened it, he glanced back at Bud. "Is this for *Raptors II*?"

Bud nodded. "ILM is doing the computer-generated imagery. I think it's going to be the best ever." He leaned against the wall, playing with the beer can in his hand. "Rumor is you're thinking of coming back and working on it."

Jason scoffed. "Rumor's wrong."

"You're sure? I mean, I'd understand if you did. Look at all the awards *Raptors* got. The sequel should have been yours."

"I'm sure." Sure he was through with special effects, miniatures, and models. The ideas weren't there anymore, the desire. He managed a smile. "Besides, you'll do a great job. Taught you all I knew, didn't I?"

"That you did."

From the day they'd met, five and a half years ago, Jason had known Bud would one day be a big name in the business. The man had talent, drive, and ambition. Lots of ambition. "Planning on winning an Oscar?"

"I sure hope so." Bud motioned toward the living room with his beer can. "By the way, where are yours?"

Jason shrugged and opened the freezer. "In one of the boxes in the extra bedroom, along with everything else I brought up. Should have dumped them."

"Oh yeah, right." Bud laughed in disbelief. "I'd have them in a showcase by the front door so everyone who came in would see them."

"Make it an airtight showcase. Karen used to say she never saw anything attract dust like they did."

For a moment there was an awkward silence, then Bud asked quietly, "Do you miss her?"

Jason groped through the packages of frozen food. He hadn't meant to bring up Karen's name, hadn't meant to start reminiscing. "I don't want to talk about her."

"You can't just block out five years of your life. Six if you include the time you two dated."

He'd like to block out three years. Three years and four months. Barely aware of what he was doing, he pushed aside a bag of peas and grabbed a package of meat. "Steaks all right?"

"Steaks are fine. Look, if you don't want to talk about Karen, we don't have to, but I'm worried about you. I can't believe you've really given up special effects and are hiding out in this ghost town—"

"Slaterville is not a ghost town. There are probably five or six hundred residents who live here year round."

"A ghost town," Bud repeated. "How could you leave Hollywood? Take off like you did? Sure, I know it was rough on you, but after a while people would have forgotten."

Jason doubted that. Karen McLain's murder was too bizarre to be forgotten. Too inexplicable. "Guess I didn't have the patience to wait that long."

Bud shook his head. "I've never seen anyone with more patience than you. I'll never forget how many days and nights you put into that one maquette for *Time Capsule*."

Jason remembered as well. Bud had been the one who'd talked him into doing that damned movie, then while he was struggling with the maquette, Bud had one-upped him and landed a better project. But there'd been a payback. "It finally worked," Jason said.

"Worked so well, it got you *Raptors*," Bud said with a hint of chagrin. "You'll be back. One of these days the urge will hit you, the creative juices will begin to flow, and the desire will return."

Jason shook his head.

"That or someone will bring you out of hiding. She liked you."

"Who liked me?" Jason asked, though he knew.

"Your lady friend. The eye doctor."

"She's not my lady friend. We just met."

"Oh yeah? Boy, when I walked in . . . the way she was looking at you and the way you were looking at her . . ." Bud shook his hand, blowing on his fingers as if trying to cool them. "It was hot."

It was crazy, that's what it was, and Jason knew it.

"You told her you'd think about helping her," Bud reminded him.

"To get her out of here."

Her presence had been too disturbing. For so long,

the only emotions he'd known had been anger and depression. He'd stopped thinking of himself as a man and lived more like a wounded animal, hiding in the dark safety of his lair, secluded from all. He hadn't expected Valerie Wiggins to come knocking on his door, to come into his house. To walk right into him.

The feel of a woman's body against his shouldn't have had such an earthshaking effect. Bud was right, though. Jason had seen the look of awareness in her eyes, heard the ragged rhythm of her breathing. His breathing had been as ragged.

It was crazy, all right. Insane.

"I told her I'd think about it. Well, I've thought about it," he said firmly. "I'm not going to help her."

Val glanced at the calendar on her office wall and realized a week had gone by since her talk with Jason. The memories—of him, his voice, his dark eyes, the feel of his body—were still so fresh, it seemed like yesterday.

"So you talked to him," the woman seated on the other side of Val's desk said. "Told him what we needed. And what did he say?"

Debbie Norrod had volunteered to work on the haunted house, and Val knew she wanted to get going on the project. Val also knew that Debbie wasn't overly enthusiastic about working with Jason. "He said he'd think about it."

"When are you going to talk to him again?"

She didn't know. She certainly didn't want to stop by his house again. Once had been enough. Jason intimidated her, but he also excited her. How she could work with him, she wasn't sure; yet she still felt he was the one who could turn their haunted house into a success.

"I'll give him a call soon," she told Debbie. "It's only mid-April. We have five and a half months until October."

"It would be great if he'd just give us some ideas."

"That's what I suggested."

Debbie leaned toward Val. "What was he like?"

Val shrugged, as if she'd hardly noticed. "Gruff. Moody." She didn't mention scary, handsome, or intriguing. "He said he was through doing special effects, that he was too busy. Maybe he is, but I don't know what he's doing. That place of his was so dark, I don't see how anyone could see to do anything."

"But before you left, he changed his mind?"

"He said he'd think about it."

"Did you notice his mouth?"

"His mouth?" Val repeated, disturbed by the question. She did remember his mouth—the sensual curve of his lips. That memory had been bothering her every night since she'd met him.

"There was a picture of him in *The Globe*," Debbie said. "One look at his mouth and I knew he did it."

"Debbie, you can't judge a man by a picture."

"Maybe you can't and maybe you can. What do you think? You've met him now. Talked to him. Did the man murder his wife?"

That was the question. Val didn't want to believe that the man who'd held her in his arms, who'd turned her thoughts to chaos and invaded her dreams since that evening, could have killed his wife. But if he was innocent, why was he living in Slaterville in a run-down house that was as dark as a tomb? "I don't know."

"Well, the possibility scares me. Maybe you think he can turn our haunted house into a big success, but I think we might be just as well off without his help."

Debbie stood and pushed back her chair. "Listen, I've got to go. The kids will be home from school soon, and I think I heard Ginger talking to someone in your waiting room. I don't want to hold you up on your appointments. Whatever you decide about the house, give me a call. I'll do something. And I think you're going to find those five and a half months go by faster than you think."

"I know." Sighing, Val rose to go out to the front desk with Debbie. She'd also heard her receptionist talking to someone. Her four-thirty appointment, probably—half an hour early. Mrs. Aitken was always early.

Mrs. Aitken also loved to talk about her most recent ailment or her uncaring children, turning half-hour appointments into hour-long lament sessions.

Val wasn't in any hurry for Debbie to leave. "See you at the next meeting?"

"Planning on it." Debbie stepped out of Val's office and into the waiting area first. She glanced toward the chairs to the left and stopped dead-still, her mouth dropping open.

A moment later Val understood.

Stepping through the doorway herself, she looked in the direction of Debbie's gaze. Wearing the same cream-colored cable-knit sweater, faded jeans, scuffed boots, and scowl that he'd worn the week before, Jason McLain sat in the chair closest to her office door.

Val's breath locked in her throat as her knees turned to butter. Quickly she grabbed the doorjamb for support. In the light of her office he seemed less menacing, yet there was still a darkness about him, an unspoken anger. Had he heard any of her conversation with Debbie? Heard their comments about his guilt or innocence?

"Mr. McLain," she said, hoping her voice didn't sound as shaky as she felt. "What a surprise."

He stood, solemnly nodding at her, then looking at Debbie, who remained immobile. Val touched her arm, and the woman jumped. "Debbie, this is Mr. McLain."

"Jason," he corrected her. "Just call me Jason."

Debbie still didn't speak, so Val went on. "Debbie is a member of the committee working on the haunted house. We were just discussing my meeting with you."

"So I heard."

"You did?" She'd hoped he hadn't.

"I, ah . . . I—I've got to go," Debbie stammered, and started toward the outside door. "Nice to have met you, Mr. McLain . . . Mr. Jason. My children . . . I need to get home, ah . . ."

Before she stepped out, she glanced back at Val. "I'll call you."

Then she was gone, and Val faced Jason, forcing a smile and not sure what to say. "She's a little shy around men."

Petrified better described the woman, Jason thought. And Val didn't look exactly relaxed herself. She'd released her death grip on the door frame, but was now shifting her weight from one foot to the other, stuffing her hands into the deep pockets of her light blue lab coat, then pulling them out again.

Why? Because she thought she was talking to a murderer?

She turned to her receptionist. "You should have told me Mr. McLain was here."

"He said not to bother you," the younger woman explained.

Val looked back at him. "I've been hoping to hear from you."

"Have you now?"

"About the haunted house."

"I'm not doing it."

She grimaced and glanced toward her office. "Because of what I said? What Debbie said?"

He shook his head.

"We really need your help."

Again he shook his head. Even before he'd stepped into her office, he'd made up his mind. What he'd overheard had merely confirmed his decision.

"It would be good publicity for you," she added.

He grimaced. "That is one thing I don't need. Look, I told you from the start, I'm through doing special effects. Any kind of special effects."

"And nothing I say will change your mind?"

"Nothing."

"Then, I guess, thank you for stopping by and telling me."

"I stopped by because I need my glasses tightened."

"Your glasses?" She frowned in confusion. He obviously wasn't wearing glasses. He held up his glasses case in explanation. "Reading glasses. They keep slipping down my nose."

"Oh."

He saw her gaze drop to the case in his hand, then lift to his eyes again, move down to his nose . . . then to his mouth. Remembering what he'd heard them saying about his mouth, he scowled.

Val quickly turned away.

Still, he saw her cheeks grow pink. He hadn't seen a woman blush in a long time. Blushing was too juvenile, too gauche, for the crowd he'd spent most of his thirty-six years with.

"Do I have time to tighten a pair of glasses?" she asked her receptionist.

"Mrs. Aitken isn't due for a half hour." The woman grinned. "Meaning she'll be here any time."

"And can wait." Val looked back at him. "Come on, we'll do your glasses."

She took him into another room, to a small table near a display of frames. Seating herself on one side, she motioned for him to take the other chair. Once he was seated, he handed her his glasses case. She carefully removed the tortoiseshell-rimmed reading glasses that he'd had for years, held them up to the light, checked the lenses, then tried the hinges. Finally she looked at him. "Let's see how they fit."

She leaned forward, holding his glasses by the earpieces, and placed them on his face. Her knuckles skimmed his temples, and the pad of her right thumb brushed over his skin. She worked with the precision of one accustomed to doing her job, yet the moment her flesh touched his, he heard her take in a quick breath and felt a moment of hesitancy.

The blue of her eyes grew deeper, and the atmosphere between them suddenly became charged. He hadn't developed an immunity to her nearness in the past week. Up close she smelled of sweetness and freshness, of femininity and promises. He could feel her warmth, the pull of her body. Sensual awareness screamed its presence, and he knew coming to see her had been a mistake.

The glasses were only an excuse. She'd brought a flicker of light into his darkened soul. He didn't want it, yet it had lingered, taunting him late into the night, hardening his body with longing.

He'd come to banish her from his thoughts. Now he realized that wasn't going to be easy. For reasons he didn't understand, that had nothing to do with physical needs, he was drawn to this woman.

"Let me tighten the hinges," she said, removing the glasses, her voice husky and a little shaky.

"Are you married?" he asked, needing to know.

She'd picked up a small screwdriver. At his question she dropped it, then hurried to pick it up again before looking at him. "No. Divorced. Why?"

"Just curious."

Was that all? Val wondered. She wished she could read his thoughts. Did he feel this energy between them? Or was it just her? It was crazy. Totally crazy. She shouldn't be acting this way. Anyone seeing her fumbling around would think she was in her first year of optometry school. What was wrong with her?

"That woman you were with," he said. "You say she's part of your group?"

"Debbie?" He'd changed the subject, and the moment was gone. Val held the glasses back up for him to try on. "Yes. I'm sorry she acted so . . . weird. She's come a long way, but she gets nervous around men she doesn't know." Val studied how his glasses rested on the bridge of his nose and fit over his ears. "Deb had a bad experience when she was nineteen. She was gang-raped at a fraternity party. She's still recovering mentally, and never did finish college. She came back up here and joined WIN. The group's really helped her a lot."

"Putting in a plug for your project?"

There was a cynicism to his tone, but she chose to ignore it. "Why not? WIN has done wonders for her. She's now happily married to a wonderful man, a widower with two children. She absolutely adores the kids, and he's so good for her. She's why our organization is important . . . why we need to make our haunted house a success. Why we need you."

"If you're trying to make me feel guilty, it's not going to work," he said. "I told you. I'm through doing gags."

"Gags?"

"Special effects. I'm through creating cute little creatures and scary monsters. I just want to be left alone."

"To hide in a house with no lights!" The moment she said it, she was sorry. Who was she to judge his behavior? Wasn't she, in a sense, hiding?

"What's the alternative?" he asked solemnly. "To have my picture plastered on the fronts of thousands of newspapers?"

"You were acquitted," she reminded him.

"*Acquitted*," he repeated, emphasizing the word. "But my wife is still dead, and the question of who killed her is still unanswered. No matter what that jury said, until her killer is caught and convicted, people are going to think I did it. So forget using me and my name. I don't want the publicity. As far as I'm concerned, for as long as I live, I don't want anyone ever mentioning my name again."

He stood and so did she, still holding his glasses. In his eyes she saw the pain, and it tore at her. "I'm sorry. We wouldn't have to use your name. All we need are ideas."

He laughed shortly. "Come on, honey. I'm from L.A., remember? The land where nobody tells the truth and everyone is using someone. It's my name that would bring people, my name that you need."

"You're wrong," she insisted.

"Am I?"

He started to leave, but she called after him. "Your glasses!"

He paused, looking back, and she slipped his glasses into their case and held them toward him. "They should fit better now."

His steps back toward her were slow, his expression guarded. "How much do I owe you?"

"Nothing." She lifted her chin, looking him directly in the eyes. "You're in Slaterville now. Here we tell the truth, and sometimes we actually do something for nothing."

"Something for nothing." He studied her face for a moment, then turned and left.

THREE

Val was busy the rest of the afternoon. Mrs. Aitken was waiting when Jason left. Val skirted the woman's curious questions about Jason, checked her eyes, and listened to her latest woes. Mrs. Aitken left just before five and Ginger went home at ten after, but Val stayed to order frames for Mrs. Bullock, the church organist, and to do a contact lens checkup for Jenny Graham, who could only come at five-thirty.

It was close to six-thirty when Val slipped into her coat, pulled the shade on her door, and stepped out of her office. For a moment she paused to inhale the fresh, crisp air of the evening and glance up at the granite peaks surrounding Slaterville. Though the snow from the week before had melted from the lower elevations, up where the Sierra Nevadas touched the heavens, the setting sun was turning the pristine white slopes to a dark purple.

"Pretty night, isn't it?"

The sound of Jason's voice surprised her, his words echoing her thoughts. Her heart was racing and the adrenaline was pumping through her body as she jerked around to face him. He was leaning against the front of the building, near the old barber shop pole. His familiar bomber jacket now covered his sweater, and his battered brown hat was pulled down low over his forehead.

"You scared me."

"Sorry." He pushed himself away from the building and took a step toward her. "I didn't mean to."

A tremor of excitement raced through her, mixed with just a dash of fear. With difficulty she tried to sound casual and relaxed. "Considering the mood you were in when you left my office, I didn't expect you to be here."

"Neither did I." He looked up and down the highway that formed the main street of the town. Except for a couple of cars driving through and a handful of people in the stores, Slaterville was deserted. "What do they do, roll up the sidewalks after six?"

"Just about. What *are* you doing here?"

"Waiting for you. Have dinner with me?"

"Dinner?"

"Why not? It's dinnertime. You have to eat. And you said you needed ideas on how to improve your haunted house." He glanced toward her office door. "I decided I was being rather egotistical earlier. My name's not essential; a good gimmick or two would bring people." He looked down the street, at the one building that did have several cars parked in front of it. "We could eat at Rosie's."

Sometimes Val stopped at Rosie's for dinner, rather than going home to an empty house and trying to decide what to cook for one person. It was convenient, and the food was reasonably priced and good. To say yes wasn't that crazy an idea, especially when Jason had implied that he'd give her ideas for the house.

It took her only a moment to agree.

Together they walked the short distance to the old building that housed Rosie's. It was just enough time for each of them to comment on the weather and complain about the snow they'd had the week before. Just enough time for Val to convince the butterflies in her stomach to stop churning and her heart to stop pounding. But not enough time for her to understand why the mere sight of Jason could send her into a tizzy.

As soon as they stepped through the restaurant's doors, they were assailed by an array of aromas, a garish decor, and the sounds of diners talking. "Two?" asked Rosie, giving Jason a curious glance before looking at Val.

Val could imagine the questions going through the woman's head. Everyone in town knew about Jason's past. Even when it wasn't headline news, gossip in Slaterville traveled fast. By tomorrow everyone would know that Valerie Wiggins had had dinner with Jason McLain.

She decided she didn't care, smiled at Rosie, and said, "Yes, two."

Rosie nodded and led them to a secluded table, leaving them with the promise that their waitress would be right there.

The building they were in dated back to the gold rush days; its walls were made of whipsawed lumber, hand-planed and nailed with hand-forged square-cut nails. Hanging here and there were relics from the 1850s—a rusty skip bucket holding an arrangement of dried flowers, a set of gold scales, a pick and a shovel.

Val was sure it was merely coincidence, but mounted on the wall behind Jason's head was a pistol. Rather than look at it, she studied her menu.

"Have you lived in Slaterville all of your life?" he asked after the young woman serving their table took their orders.

"No. I was born and raised in Sacramento."

"You moved from Sacramento to here?" The lift of his eyebrows expressed his surprise.

Others had been even more surprised when she'd accepted the job, but the move had been necessary. "I like the area," she said honestly. "What about you? You moved from Hollywood to Slaterville. Why here instead of . . . New York?"

"New York," he repeated, then scoffed at the idea. "I wanted someplace quiet. Someplace where I could . . ."

He hesitated, but she had a feeling she already knew. In a way, his reason was no different than hers. "Someplace where you could hide?" she finished for him.

Just the hint of a smile touched his mouth. "Right. Anyway, I remembered this area from years back when I worked on a movie up here. *Ghost Miners of the Sierra Nevadas.* You probably didn't see it. It was pretty bad."

"I saw the video. It's popular around here because people still remember when it was filmed. And as bad as the plot was, the special effects were great."

His grin grew wider. "It was a learning experience . . . and I did like being up here. When the realtor I contacted said there was a house for sale in this town, I grabbed it."

"And probably paid too much." At least that was what she'd heard. "That house was in pretty bad shape."

"Still is," he admitted. "I suppose I should fix it up some."

"It could be pretty."

His gaze played over her face, and she wondered what he was thinking. What she was thinking was crazy. Here she should be concentrating on asking him for ideas for the haunted house; instead, she wanted to know more about him. How had he gotten the small, white scar close to his temple? Did he find it lonely living by himself? Was his pulse racing as fast as hers?

At first she'd thought her fascination with him was merely because of the unanswered questions regarding his wife's death. But if that was all it was, why then did she find herself staring at his mouth and wondering what his kisses would be like?

He smiled, and she realized her gaze was locked on his lips. Quickly she looked away.

"You work long hours," he said softly, and she glanced back.

"Not really. Tonight I was simply later than usual. Besides, I love my job."

"That's good." This time it was his gaze that drifted to her mouth. "You said you're divorced?"

The muscles in her stomach tightened, and her breath locked in her lungs. "Yes."

"A recent event or . . . ?"

She supposed it depended on how you looked at it. "My divorce was final ten years ago."

"Ten years?" He lifted his eyebrows. "You must have been a child bride."

Childish, she would definitely agree. Immature. "I was seventeen, right out of high school and certain that love would conquer all."

"He abused you?"

The directness of the question surprised her and took her off guard. "Why do you ask that?"

"You're connected with this Women In Need group."

"Maybe I'm just the volunteer type."

"If you don't want to talk about it, that's all right."

She didn't want to talk about it, but not talking would prove Mike still had a hold on her. She tried to appear casually indifferent and gave a shrug. "It's no big deal. Yes, Mike abused me."

For a moment Jason said nothing, yet she sensed that her words had bothered him. When he did speak, his voice was gentle.

"So you left him?"

"And left him and left him." Even now she hated herself for that weakness, for going back, even when she should have known better. "Thank goodness there was a safe house in Sacramento to go to."

"Another plug for safe houses?" Jason asked, smiling and sitting back as the waitress brought their salads to the table.

"Why not?"

Val waited until they were again alone before she went on. "I wouldn't be an optometrist if it hadn't been for the help I got there. Not just emotional help, but those women became my friends. They helped me out financially, found me a permanent place to live. I am what I am today because of them, and that's why I don't want to see the safe house we have up here fail because of a lack of funds. Do you understand?"

Jason was beginning to. He could understand what had brought her to his door, had made her ask for his help. Understand her zealous fervor to make a project succeed.

He also understood he needed to stay far, far away from her. She was making him care, was getting past the barriers he'd erected . . . bringing him back to life.

And that could be dangerous.

He'd left her office ready to wipe her from his thoughts. Only he couldn't. Since moving to Slaterville, he'd rarely spent more than an hour in town, but he'd waited over two hours for her to leave her office. Had waited, his hat pulled down so it almost hid his face, and endured the stares of the people who'd walked by, the whispered comments they'd shared after they'd passed. Waited and chided himself for his foolishness, told himself to leave, to go back to the sanctuary of his dark, barren house. Yet he'd stayed.

"So tell me about this haunted house," he said.

"What do you want to know?"

"What you—your group—have done in the past."

"The usual. Played scary music, created a few ghosts out of sheets and pulleys, hung some sheets to make a maze and some string so it felt like walking through spider webs, and had volunteers dressed in costumes jump out and make scary noises at appropriate times. The first year I was here, people loved what we had. But last year we heard a lot of kids say it wasn't scary enough, and attendance was definitely down. With more and more groups doing this every Halloween, I'm afraid we aren't going to get enough people coming to ours to make any money."

"Unless you have a few gimmicks," he said, certain she was right. Kids and grown-ups alike were too used to sophisticated, computerized special effects. What might have worked a decade before was now too tame. "Where's this house located?"

"It's the old Clifford place, south of town. The fifth house on the left before you get to the sign that says Slaterville. The one set back from the road."

He'd seen it, and the place was perfect for a haunted house. There was a broken-down picket fence in front, a wooden-plank walkway leading up to a wide porch, and a massive wooden door. Two stories high in front and built into the hillside, it was sided in weather-beaten wood. Half of the shutters hung on a slant, and the house was surrounded by old, gnarled trees. Behind the house, farther up the hill, was an equally dilapidated-looking outbuilding.

"Structurally the place is safe?" he asked.

"Except for the floor in one room. Sheriff Maxwell went through the whole house and checked it out for us. All was fine until he stamped on the floorboards in the game room. He almost fell through to a cellar we didn't even know existed. We have that room closed off, but hope to get the floor fixed this year."

Jason leaned forward, his interest piqued. "There's a cellar?"

She took a bite of salad and nodded. "You get to it through a trapdoor. We didn't find that until after the sheriff nearly fell through. The whole house is very un-usual, but then, Eldon Clifford, it seems, was a very unusual man. He built the house himself and is reputed to have held nightly poker games that drew people from all parts of the country. One very influential San Fran-cisco politician was never seen again after playing cards at the house. Clifford was questioned, but no one could prove anything."

Jason smiled fleetingly. "I see certain parallels there."

"I hope not too many," she said, frowning. "Eldon Clifford was killed in that house. They say it was a disgruntled gambler who shot him."

"And do they say he now haunts the house?"

She shook her head and grinned. "No, but we've been circulating that tale. I mean, why not? We are trying to get people to come to a haunted house."

Why not, indeed? Jason was beginning to get an idea. "You only open this house during the month of October?"

"Just a couple of weeks before Halloween. There's really nothing else we can use it for during the year."

"And you own it?"

"The group does. A Thomas Barclay bought the house in 1924. His wife, Edna Barclay, was one of the founders of WIN. When she died, she willed the property to the organization."

"The question is," Jason asked, "is it a windfall or an albatross?"

"Any ideas on how to make it a windfall?"

He actually had a couple, which surprised him. It had been over three years since he'd had a creative thought, three years since he'd allowed himself to do anything but wallow in self-pity and question his sanity. It was difficult to remember how he'd been back before Karen's death.

For four months before her death he'd been in England, setting up some special effects for *Raptors*, overseeing the construction of the barriers that would ultimately collapse and the towers that would explode. In spite of all the problems and accidents that occurred there, he'd returned to the States eager to finish the movie and get to work on a new project. He'd even considered starting his own company. But that was before he'd learned that his wife hadn't missed him nearly as much as he'd missed her during the months he'd been gone, before the insanity had taken over his life.

The horror of it all—Karen's murder, his own arrest, the trial—and the unanswered questions that haunted him had blotted out all his creativity. But now, as he gazed across the table at a woman he barely knew, his head was full of ideas—though only a few had anything to do with making a house scary for Halloween.

A relationship with a woman—with Valerie Wiggins —was the last thing he should be thinking of. He'd come to Slaterville to hide from his emotions, to simply exist. Only he couldn't live that way anymore. From the night Val had knocked on his door, his life had changed.

"Why you?" he asked.

She was clearly confused. "Me?"

"How did you get picked to knock on my door?"

Her smile and shrug came at the same time. "Just lucky, I guess."

"In other words, the others were afraid to talk to me."

Solemnly she nodded.

"But not you?"

"Oh, I was—" She hesitated, and he waited. "Nervous," she finished with a grin.

"I think you were scared to death."

She laughed, and he basked in the warmth of the sound. It had been so long since he'd heard laughter, so long since he'd allowed himself to smile. He was smiling now, had been most of the evening.

"I lived through it, didn't I?" she said, and reached across the table to touch his hand. "Though I thought you were going to take off my head when you first opened that door and glared at me. I do like it better when you smile."

He caught her fingers in his, gently holding them. Her eyes seemed to darken; the pull between them strengthened. He was the one who was afraid now. "You don't really know me."

"No, I don't," she agreed, her voice husky.

"I could be some sort of a monster."

"You could be." She stared into his eyes, and he could feel her tension. Then she laughed and squeezed his fingers. "Or a hero who's going to save our haunted house."

He chuckled and released her hand. "You never give up, do you? All right, tell me more about this haunted house and your group."

As they ate Val talked freely about WIN, her work with the organization, and her involvement with the haunted house project. It was her personal life she avoided discussing, just as they skirted around anything that touched on his life before he'd moved to Slaterville. They also talked about the town, and by the time they'd finished their meal, their conversation had switched to the gold rush days.

"Can't you just picture how it was back then?" Val asked as they walked from the restaurant toward her office and their vehicles. "They say in the 1850s there were close to six thousand people living in or around Slaterville. The streets sure wouldn't have been this dead at night."

Actually, Val thought, the quiet was eerie, especially

the farther they walked from Rosie's. She shivered and pulled her coat closer.

"Cold?" Jason asked.

"A little," she admitted, not sure if the shiver running down her spine was due to the temperature or the realization of how alone she was with him. Alone to face her feelings.

He wrapped an arm around her shoulders, drawing her closer to his side and the warmth of his body. She took in a breath and held it, the scent of him filling her. Hypothermia was no danger, not as fast as her heart was now beating. A liquid heat surged through her, igniting thoughts better left dormant.

"They say we're supposed to have temperatures warmer than normal this spring," she said, needing to talk.

"That so?"

She wasn't sure, but his voice sounded huskier than earlier, his words throatier. Was it possible he was feeling the same reactions she was?

Step by step, she walked beside him, absorbing his warmth and his strength. She'd spent less than two hours with him, yet the doubts she'd once held about his guilt or innocence were gone. Without reason or proof, she knew Jason McLain wasn't responsible for the death of his wife. Her only fears were of the future, of taking a chance and failing. She'd done that once too many times.

"Do you have any ideas?" she asked, wanting to get her mind and the conversation back on track.

His deep chuckle told her she'd phrased her question wrong. Perhaps a Freudian slip. "About the haunted house," she quickly added.

"A few."

That was all he said.

Above them a sliver of moon slid in and out of a veil of clouds. The wind whispered its eerie call through the pines and cedars. Not a person could be seen, no cars on the road.

Even in the gravel parking lot where she'd left her car, the only other vehicle was Jason's Jeep. When they reached her car, Val stepped away. Jason caught her hand before she opened her car door. "Are you still . . . nervous?"

She faced him. "I guess that depends on how you define nervous."

"You don't really know me."

From all she'd read, she probably knew him better than most of the men she'd ever dated. "Do we ever truly know another person?"

"No," he said with a sadness that conveyed a meaning deeper than she understood. He tentatively touched the side of her face. "Thank you for having dinner with me."

She swallowed hard, hoping he couldn't hear the wild beating of her heart. "I enjoyed it."

"So did I."

With his fingertips he traced the contour of her jaw, and even in the darkness she felt the intensity of his gaze. "Your skin's soft," he murmured.

And his fingertips were coarse, she thought, but she loved the feel of them, the ragged sound of his breathing, the musky, leathery smell of his jacket.

"I haven't been out with a woman for a long time, not since . . ."

He didn't finish, but she understood.

"I should say good night," he continued, but didn't. Instead, he moved his hand to her hair, combing his finger into her curls.

That she wanted him to kiss her was crazy. That she thought he might, took her breath away. "Jason?" she whispered.

His "yes" was barely audible.

He stood perfectly still, his hand no longer moving, and she knew the decision was hers. Reaching up, she touched the sleeves of his jacket, her fingers gripping the age-softened leather.

She watched as his face drew nearer, the brim of his hat obliterating moon and clouds from her view. The brush of his lips was no more than a tempting promise, then he pulled back, watching her . . . waiting for her response.

She didn't know what to say. All reason had long ago escaped her mind. Haunted houses. A murdered wife. Women in need. None of it mattered. Only her desire to know his kisses, to feel his arms around her and forget everything but the moment.

"Yes," she pleaded, asking for more.

He gave, his mouth taking hers, all hesitancy gone. The promise was fulfilled, and she clung to him, leaning into his body, feeling the heat of him through the thickness of their coats, and the hardness of him through the touch of his hips. To know that she excited him aroused her.

He teased her mouth, and she parted her lips, moving them with his. At the touch of his tongue, she opened more, giving him access. Reality was gone, sensations taking precedent over everything.

Deep inside, her muscles tightened, and a small

moan escaped her lips. He combed his fingers deeper into her hair and held her closer. Breathing became impossible; she heard small gasps in the night. They were two, yet they were one, their kisses blending and their needs the same.

A car passed through town, the stroke of its headlights catching them unaware. It was there and then it was gone, moving on up the mountainside and out of the realm of their world. Val wasn't even sure they'd been seen, yet that moment of light had pierced the illusion.

Jason's lips froze against hers, and she sucked in a breath. He straightened, keeping her close, and she rested her cheek against his jacket and listened to the pounding of his heart. Silently she questioned her sanity. Here she was kissing a man she barely knew, making out in a public parking lot. As the sensuality that had driven her faded, the reality of what she'd done frightened her.

"This is crazy," he said, his voice a rumbling echo of her thoughts.

"I know."

"I didn't mean for it to happen."

Nor had she. How did you explain the unexplainable?

Ever so slowly his breathing became normal, the thud of his heart even, and she could feel the same changes in her own body. How long they stood beside her car, his arms wrapped around her, holding her close to his warmth and protecting her from the wind and the view of anyone driving by, she wasn't sure. Finally, though, he loosened his hold and drew back. "You all right?"

"Fine." She shrugged, afraid to say much more. She was all right if insanity was all right. All right if wanting what you shouldn't have was all right. She studied his face, trying to understand what had happened to her—to them.

"Maybe it's spring fever," he said, almost in answer to her confusion.

"Must be." She was willing to accept any reason.

"I didn't come up here to get involved . . . with anyone."

"I understand."

"I can't. I shouldn't. I came up here to . . . to . . ."

"To hide," she said, and managed a small laugh. Feeling stronger, she pulled back, away from his touch. "The problem with small towns is you can't hide. Sooner or later someone comes knocking on your door asking you to get involved."

"It wouldn't—"

She didn't let him finish. "Involved with a haunted house. That's all I want."

He chuckled. "You never give up, do you?"

"Not when it's something I believe in."

"I'll think about it."

She'd heard that before, yet this time she had more hope.

FOUR

Val didn't see or hear from Jason for a week, but she thought about him often. She thought about the day she'd gone to his house and the day he'd come to her office. She thought about the dinner they'd shared . . . and the kiss.

Over and over she remembered that kiss. She analyzed the moments that had led up to it, her desires, and her reactions. Ever since moving to Slaterville, she'd been careful not to repeat past errors. No more involvements with abusive men. No more letting her emotions rule her head. No more being a victim. She was the one in control of her destiny.

But she hadn't been in control that night.

When it came to Jason, she wondered if she'd ever been in control. From the first time she'd seen his picture in the newspaper, three years ago, she'd been fascinated. His dark, haunting eyes had held her transfixed. The accusations and story had piqued her curiosity.

Had the man killed his wife?

The night they'd had dinner, she'd decided the answer was no. On an instinctive, emotional level, she still didn't think he had, but there was a place in the logical part of her mind that continued to raise the question. And so did others.

"So what do you think, Val?" her receptionist asked the following Wednesday morning. "Did that McLain guy get away with murder?"

"I don't think so. But who knows."

"Debbie's sure he did. She stopped by last Thursday, when you were down working at the clinic in Grass Valley, to make sure you were all right and to find out what he'd wanted." Ginger paused and smiled knowingly. "I didn't tell her he was waiting outside the office when I left Wednesday night."

Val laughed. "She probably already knew. I'm sure Rosie and everyone else in town have spread the word that I had dinner with him that night. I swear, around here people know what you're doing faster than you do."

"Then Debbie will probably be in this afternoon to check on why he was here this morning."

"Jason—I mean, Mr. McLain—was here this morning?" That information took Val by surprise.

"No, but he just called for an appointment, and I slipped him into your eleven o'clock cancellation. He wants a complete eye exam. That was all right, wasn't it?"

"Fine," Val said, and glanced at her watch. One hour until she saw him again, gazed into those eyes that fascinated her so. One hour to get her pulse back to normal and quell the queasy feeling inside.

How should she act?

How would he act?

One hour later Val stepped into the reception area and Ginger handed her Jason's file, including the information sheet he'd just filled out. "Mr. McLain," Val said formally. "If you'll come with me?"

He smiled and stood, saying nothing as he followed her into her examining room. She motioned to the chair next to her equipment and closed the door. It wasn't until he'd seated himself and she stepped nearer that he spoke. " 'Mr. McLain'?" he said. "I thought we were on more familiar terms than that."

She could feel the heat of a blush in her cheeks and tried to ignore it. "I wasn't sure how you wanted to be addressed in front of others."

"Ah," he said. Nothing more.

She glanced over his file, trying to concentrate on what he'd written. He was watching her with those brooding eyes of his, and she prayed she looked more composed than she felt. She scanned the personal information he'd given; there was little that she didn't already know. The man was thirty-six, a widower, no allergies and on no medications.

Finally she looked up. "Did you bring your reading glasses?"

"Yes." He pulled the case from his shirt pocket. "What you did last week helped. No more slipping."

"Good." She took the glasses he offered, carefully keeping her fingers from touching his. She knew what physical contact with this man could do to her. It was unnerving.

The day she'd tightened his frames, she'd made a rough estimate of his degree of correction. This time she conducted a more thorough examination, jotting notes in his file. Unless his vision had deteriorated, he had a mild degree of hyperopia, nothing more.

"I've been thinking about your haunted house," he said. "And about us."

She put the glasses down and faced him. "And?"

"I have some ideas. There are a few things that you and the others in your group could set up on your own, but I think if you really want your haunted house to be spectacular, you're going to have to expand beyond the usual gimmicks."

"I agree."

"Which means you'll need my help."

She nodded. "That's why I came to you."

"If I'm not mistaken," he said gravely, "you came because the others were afraid to. Chances are, you're the one who's going to end up working with me. I want you to be sure."

"Meaning?"

"Meaning, this is a small town. People talk."

"That's a given."

"I was accused of killing my wife."

"The question is, did you?"

"I told the police I didn't."

It wasn't an answer. Not that she'd thought he would admit it if he had. "And what are you telling me?"

His gaze was unwavering. "That you'll be safe. That nothing will happen."

She wondered how she could be safe when simply being close to him had her teetering on the edge. How could nothing happen when simply looking into his eyes had her pulse rate in the danger zone? Still, she tried to sound in control. "I never thought anything different," she said. "Shall we check your vision?"

Jason sat patiently, doing whatever she asked as she checked his peripheral vision, then had him read from the chart. Every so often she made more notes in his file. Throughout the examination she was temptingly close, yet tauntingly far away. He wanted to reach out and touch her, but forced himself to grip the armrests of the chair instead. Even when she placed drops in his eyes, she treated him as any other patient, slipping on latex gloves and barely touching him.

He knew he shouldn't complain, yet he wanted to. The moment she left him alone, saying she needed to give the drops time to work, he swore under his breath. For a week he'd been fighting the desire to see her again. Every day, he'd told himself to forget working with her, to forget her. Every night, he'd tossed and turned in bed, remembering the feel of her pressed against his body, the taste of her and the warmth of her.

He wasn't sure when he'd given up the fight. Perhaps the day before, when he'd begun jotting down possible ideas for her haunted house. Perhaps that morning, when he'd called and asked if he could get an appointment.

He'd told himself he just wanted to see her again, talk to her, and that her office would be a safe place to meet. It seemed he was right. She was being so careful to keep her distance, it was almost amusing.

Almost.

He had his eyes closed when she came back into the room. Immediately he opened them.

"Tired?" she asked.

"A little." And she was to blame for that. Thinking about her had not been conducive to sleep.

"When was the last time you had your eyes examined?" She checked his to see if they'd dilated.

"Four . . . five years ago." He'd forgotten exactly when. Definitely before his life had turned upside down.

"Any problems?"

Too many to list, he thought, but since none of them had anything to do with his eyes, he merely shook his head. "I only need glasses when I read and do close work. Otherwise I can see fine."

She slipped on a face mask and sat on a stool in front of him. "I'm going to check your eye pressure."

"You need a mask?" he asked.

Not even looking at him, she pulled her equipment into place. "Nowadays it's standard procedure."

He chuckled at the irony. "Valerie, you kissed me last week."

Her gaze jumped to the closed door, then to his face. "That was different," she said, her voice lowered. Above the mask her cheeks were tinged pink.

"I don't have AIDS or any communicable diseases," he said, touching her arm.

His fingertips could have been hot pokers, the way she jerked back. Her arm hit a tray, sending it to the floor with a clatter. Val gasped, staring at the fallen tray, then at him.

The door flew open, and her receptionist burst into the room. "What happened?"

"Nothing," Val said too quickly. "He . . . I—" She stopped herself. "I knocked over a tray."

Ginger's glance moved between the two of them, finally settling on Val. "You okay?"

"Fine . . . fine." She knelt down and began picking up the eyeglass frames that had been on the tray. "Everything's under control."

Ginger slowly stepped out of the room, her gaze still jumping between the two of them. As the door closed Val put the tray back on the counter. Jason waited until she was again seated in front of him before he asked, "And *is* everything under control?"

"Yes," she said firmly, and took in a deep breath. "You surprised me."

"And you surprised me. Where's that warm, responsive woman I kissed last week?"

"That was . . . I mean . . ." She stammered to a halt.

"A mistake?"

She wouldn't look him in the eyes, and her "yes" was barely audible.

He knew she was right, it had been a mistake. His body wasn't agreeing, though. "Meaning hands off?"

She still wouldn't look at him. "I . . . ah, think it would be best."

Liar, he wanted to yell, but only smiled. Maybe a good actress could hide her emotions, but Valerie Wiggins wasn't a good actress. He could see how he affected her.

He knew how she affected him.

It wouldn't take much to change her mind, except her decision was for the best. Hands off.

It was the safest way.

"So be it," he said, folding his hands in his lap.

Val finished testing his eyes, checking for signs of glaucoma and measuring the degree of his farsightedness. Finally she took off the mask and jotted down her diagnosis. "Your left eye shows some change, but I don't think it's enough to prescribe new glasses . . . unless you're having problems."

"Just with the frames slipping. And you fixed that."

"In that case . . ." She closed his file. "You're done. Your eyes will be sensitive for a while, but we'll give you some dark glasses to wear."

He stood and she handed him a slip of paper. "Give this to Ginger, and she'll let you know what you owe and give you the dark glasses. Now, about the haunted house?"

"I want a guided tour of the place."

"Whenever you'd like." Picking up a bottle of alcohol and a wipe, she began cleaning her equipment.

"Tonight?"

Val stopped her cleaning and stared at him. "Tonight?"

"Around eight o'clock?"

She hesitated. "It's dark at eight, and we don't have the electricity on in the house."

"Flashlights?"

Flashlights, she supposed, would work. She certainly wasn't going to tell him she was afraid of the dark. Lacking another excuse, she nodded. "I guess . . . as long as some of the committee are available."

He shook his head. "I don't want a committee, not yet. I want *you* to show me around, explain what's there and how it works."

"Just me?"

She knew the quaver in her voice had relayed her nervousness. Especially when he smiled. "You are the one who came to see me, aren't you? The one who started all of this?"

She tried to think of a quick excuse why she couldn't do it. To her dismay, none came to mind. She sighed with reluctance. "I guess I'll be there."

"Shall I pick you up at your place?"

"No." Just in case she needed it, she wanted a ready escape available—her car. "I, ah—I may have to run an errand beforehand. I'll meet you there at the house."

He nodded, still smiling, and left. Val watched him leave, cursing herself for acting like an idiot. Here he'd agreed to help, was doing exactly what she'd asked, and she was panicking.

What was wrong with her? Every time he touched her, she jumped like an electrified cat. Simply being in the same room with him had her pulse rate soaring. She'd tried to act normal throughout his eye exam, but knew she'd failed miserably. And now she was going to meet him in a scary old house with no electricity. Be alone with him in the dark.

Alone, Val repeated to herself eight hours later when she pulled up next to the Clifford place. Jason's Jeep was already parked in the gravel lot, and she could see the jiggling beam of a flashlight upstairs in the back bedroom. How Jason had gotten into the house, she didn't know. She'd thought Debbie and she had the only keys, besides the one in the WIN files.

Val grabbed the flashlight in her glove compartment, tested it for brightness, then got out of her car. The night was cool and as dark as dark could be, clouds blocking out the moon and stars. From somewhere up the side of the mountain an owl hooted, adding to the goosebumps already covering her skin. She pulled her coat closer.

Each step she took along the wooden-plank walkway

echoed into the night, then she heard another sound—a faint screeching—and paused. Looking around, she trailed her beam of light over the grassy stubble that had survived the winter and across the gnarled trunks of the oaks surrounding the house, their twisted limbs stretching like shriveled arms toward the sky. Had a branch rubbed against a window?

Or had she heard something else?

It might take more to scare today's teenagers, but she was shaking inside.

She expected the front door to be open, and was surprised when she found it still locked. She fished the key from her purse, then opened the door and stepped inside. "Jason?" she called up the stairway ahead of her. "You up there?"

Silence met her question, along with the smell of dust and stale air. She sneezed, then called out again. "Jason?"

She thought she heard a creak and a thump coming from the closet near the base of the stairs. Blood pounding in her ears, she swung her flashlight in that direction.

Again, from inside the closet, she heard a thump.

Over the years, she'd seen dozens of movies about haunted houses, and with every one, she'd railed at the heroines for opening doors and putting themselves in danger. How stupid each had seemed.

Her legs shaking and her heart in her throat, Val crossed the entryway to the closet door. Staring at the doorknob, she hesitated. Should she open it?

Another thing those old movies always had were people in closets, bound and gagged and crumpled on the floor. Those were just fantasies. This could be for real.

It could be Jason.

Quickly, before she lost her nerve, Val opened the door.

Jason stood with his back to her, running the palm of his right hand over the boards at the rear of the closet. He filled most of the area, and all she could see was the back of his battered brown hat, his bomber jacket, blue jeans, and boots.

For a moment he continued running his fingers over the boards, then he faced her. "Very interesting."

"Interesting?" She stared at the knotty pine wall he'd been touching, seeing nothing particularly interesting. "I heard thumping."

"That was me."

"Did you come alone?"

A lift of his eyebrows expressed his question. "Yes."

"Then there's someone else in the house. When I pulled up outside, I saw a light upstairs."

He chuckled. "Just me. Come on in."

He squeezed back, against a side wall, leaving barely enough room for her to fit inside the closet. She hesitated. "Why?"

"Because I want to show you something."

Her imagination played with that idea, triggering butterflies in her stomach. His sexy smile didn't help. "How did you get into the house anyway?"

"I'll show you." He continued grinning. "If you'll come in here."

"Can't you just tell me?"

"Afraid?"

Yes, her mind cried. Of the dark, of you and how you

make me feel. "No," she said, and swallowing hard, she stepped into the closet.

The sleeve of her wool coat rubbed against the sleeve of his jacket. She scrunched herself against the far wall, but there was no getting away from him. He dominated the small space.

"Notice anything?" he asked.

She noticed her heart was racing so fast, she was almost dizzy; that their two flashlights gave the closet a golden glow; and that he smelled masculine and clean, a mixture of leather and spice. She also noticed another smell. A damp, musty odor.

As he had, she touched the back wall. The boards were dry. Curious, she glanced up at his face. "What should I notice?"

"Feel along the edge of those two boards." He pointed at two in front of her, and she moved her fingers in that direction. "Feel anything?"

She did. "There's a slight gap between them. Very slight, but definitely a gap."

"Now bring your hand down to the middle of the wall and a little to your right."

She did as he'd instructed, but felt nothing.

"No, more to your right." He didn't wait for her to move her hand, but placed his own on top of hers, guiding her fingers to where he wanted them.

She held her breath, more aware of the feel of his rough, warm palm than of anything under her hand. Not until she felt the rise of a knot in the wood did her thoughts return to the wall. "I feel it," she said.

"Good. Now push."

She pushed and gasped. With the creak of rusty hinges, the wall in front of her opened away from them, letting in a cool blast of air and a musty aroma. Jason pushed the door all the way open, and Val focused her flashlight on what was beyond.

What she saw was a space about three feet deep and a wall of dirt and stone. The opening from the closet was narrow, but wide enough for Jason to have passed through. Without moving, she looked at him. "What is it?"

"An underground passageway. You didn't know about it?"

"I had no idea." She kept her light directed into the empty space. "How did you find it?"

"By accident. I came over a couple of hours ago and started looking around the outside. The building out back was open, and I was checking it out. I got curious when I noticed its outside dimensions were greater than the space inside, so I figured there was a room or something that I hadn't seen. When I started looking, I found a doorway like this one behind some old timbers leaning against one wall. Even with the boards moved, it wasn't easy to find the latch that opened it, but once I did . . . voilà! Step inside."

She did so, hesitantly. He followed, dominating the space and pushing her farther into the passageway. She scanned the area around her with her light, noticing the passageway traveled to her left and stone steps led up to her right. "That way leads to the building out back?" She pointed her light to the left.

"All underground. And the steps lead upstairs to the back bedroom."

"So you were up there when I arrived."

"I saw you pull up and thought I'd greet you by popping out of the closet when you opened the front door. But I had trouble getting the door down here to open again. By the time I succeeded, you were already inside, yelling for me."

"I can't believe we never found this." She ran her hand along the cold slate that lined the walls. "Every year we clean this place. It seems like someone would have hit that knot before and opened the door."

With a slight pressure from his hand, he guided her farther into the passageway, away from the door. She turned to watch him close it, a panicky feeling surging through her as the door clicked shut. Too many times as a child, she'd been locked in the closet for being bad. From what she'd read, she'd fared better than some children who'd suffered the same punishment. She didn't consider herself claustrophobic, but she didn't like small places, especially not small, dark places where doors might not open again, and where the man standing beside her both excited and scared her. Her hand tightened around her flashlight.

"See there?" Jason directed the beam of his flashlight midway down the wooden doorframe. Two holders were nailed to the wood. Then he moved the light to a board leaning against the wall. "I found that board in those holders. It would have kept the door from opening even if the knot was pushed. My guess, from what you told me, is our Mr. Eldon Clifford dug out all of this the same time he dug that cellar you were telling me about. Probably as a quick escape if one of his poker games got a little too tense. After he died, someone found the passageway and sealed this door and the one upstairs. Want to go up?" He waved his light in the direction of the steps. "That door opens easily."

"Sure," she said, definitely not liking the closed space they were in.

With one hand against the wall for stability and her other hand gripping her flashlight, she kept the beam directed on the stone steps that rose steeply in front of her. Though he didn't touch her, she could feel Jason right behind her. She didn't know why they needed any special effects in this house. It was scaring her just as it was—hidden doorways, secret passages, and darkness.

Something brushed against her cheek, and she squealed and jerked back, losing her balance. Her hand banged against the wall, and she dropped her flashlight. Jason grabbed her from behind, his hands spanning her waist.

"My light!" she gasped, trying to ignore how her hips were now pressed against Jason's abdomen and his fingers were right under her breasts. She was glad for all the clothing she wore. The position was way too intimate.

Using his flashlight, he scanned the stairs. Her flashlight lay against the stones two steps above her.

The moment Jason released her, she moved away, letting out the breath she'd held. She could feel how her nipples had hardened. The slightest touch and he had her quivering.

Quickly she reached for her light. She tried the on and off switch several times, but with no success. "Must have broken something," he said, taking it from her and dropping it into his jacket pocket. "What scared you?"

"Something brushed against my face." She shivered, remembering.

"That's all?"

"It was enough," she said, angry with herself for reacting so foolishly. Now she'd lost her light.

He cast the beam of his flashlight around the passageway, illuminating several lacy cobwebs hanging from above. Another shiver ran down her spine. "I'm afraid of spiders," she said.

He touched her hand. Nerves on edge, she jerked back, then wished she hadn't. His quick intake of breath relayed his own reaction, and she could almost feel him draw into himself.

"Sure it's spiders you're afraid of?" he asked coolly.

"Spiders," she insisted. "And the dark."

He snorted in disbelief. "You wouldn't be just a little 'nervous' about being alone with a murderer, would you?"

"Of course not," she lied. "You said you didn't do it."

"I said I told the police I didn't do it. I could have lied."

A possibility she'd considered more than once. "I read all about the trial. You were acquitted. You had no motive."

He was silent for a moment, then asked, "And what if I did have a motive?"

FIVE

The icy chill that ran through Val wasn't caused by a fear of spiders or the dark. Jason's question was too ominous, his voice too level. Like a punch to the stomach, it took her breath away.

Could she have been wrong about him?

Was he a murderer?

For three years she'd convinced herself that no man would kill the woman he loved without a motive. No matter what the media had said, a part of her had always believed in his innocence. Now . . .

"And what was your motive?" she asked, wishing her body would stop shaking.

"Jealousy," he said with deadly calm. "The day before my wife was shot, she told me she'd had an affair with another man."

"How come that never came out in the trial?" Not once had she read anything about another man.

"Because I didn't tell anyone . . . nor did the other man. So what do you think now, Dr. Valerie Wiggins? Are you still so sure I didn't murder my wife?"

"I think you're trying to scare me." And he was doing a damned good job of it.

"*I'm* scaring you? Let's be honest, Val, you've been afraid from the day you first came to my house. The question has always been there, lurking in the back of your mind. Did he kill his wife?"

"No," she said. "You're wrong. I—"

He turned off the flashlight, and she gasped. "What are you doing?"

"Saving energy."

In the inky darkness she had to forget her eyes and rely on her other senses. Just the slightest of sounds alerted her that he'd moved. "Jason?"

"What?" he asked, his warm breath fanning her neck.

He was right behind her, only inches away. She could reach back and touch him if she wanted, grab onto him for security. She clenched her hands to her sides. "You're not playing fair."

"And what game are we playing? Shall we call it Trust? Do you trust me, Valerie?"

"Yes," she said, then sucked in a quick breath when his hand touched the side of her neck.

His short laugh held no humor. "I don't think so. Trust implies faith, faith that I won't hurt you. And that's not there, is it? You were afraid when you stepped into that closet with me, and now you're about to run."

"I'm not running anywhere," she said honestly. Her shaking legs wouldn't get her up the steps fast enough to escape a flea. "And I do trust you, it's just—"

He sighed and snapped the light back on, once again illuminating the stairs. "Never mind. Let's get out of here."

Her legs rubbery and her body trembling, Val made her way to the top. Occasionally a cobweb brushed against her face. It didn't bother her any longer.

At the top Jason pressed a latch, then drew her back, close to his body. She didn't object. Confusion ruled her thinking, reason and emotion at war. A narrow door swung open, and he guided her into another closet. When he closed the door behind him, she glanced back. This entry was as invisible as the one downstairs.

He followed her into the bedroom. There he handed her his flashlight. "You take this. I'm leaving."

Dumbfounded, she watched him head for the bedroom door. He was out of the room and into the upstairs hallway before she shook off the stupor and hurried after him. "Jason, wait!"

She caught him with the beam of her light at the top of the stairs. "Wait for what?" he demanded, facing her.

"I do trust you . . . and I know you didn't kill your wife."

"How do you know that?"

"Because—because you wouldn't." There was no logic to it. It was a gut feeling.

"Then maybe you know more than I do."

"Maybe."

He turned and started back toward her. "You were scared in there."

"Yes," she admitted. "I told you, I'm scared of the dark. I have been ever since I was a child. And I'm scared of spiders . . . and of cobwebs and of being in enclosed places."

"And scared of me?" He stopped, halfway between the stairs and her.

"No—yes." She took in a deep breath, deciding the

truth was better than clouds of doubt. "I'm not in control when I'm around you."

"And you want to be in control?"

"Of how I feel."

He smiled wryly and took another step toward her. "Well, if it helps, I'm not in control of how I feel when I'm around you. Otherwise I wouldn't even be here."

She watched him come closer. The glow from the flashlight cast shadows on the wall, and his grew larger, more ghoulish and frightening with each step he took. She knew she was scaring herself again. With a flick, she snapped off the light.

"Why'd you do that?" Jason asked.

"Maybe it's time I stop being afraid," she said, but she heard the tremor in her voice.

"Maybe you should be afraid." He chuckled, low and suggestive.

"Now who's playing games?"

"Good question."

She sensed he was only inches away and waited for him to touch her. Every sound in the room was magnified. His breathing. Hers. The rustling of his jacket as he moved his arm. She felt his hand brush against the side of her coat. Boldly she stepped forward.

He stopped her before her body touched his. "Don't you want to put on a face mask?"

"No."

"Latex gloves?"

"Jason . . ."

He ran his hands up and down her sleeves, rubbing her arms. "I know. You were just doing your job." He drew her closer, enfolding her in his embrace.

"It has nothing to do with fear."

"It has everything to do with fear," he said firmly. "Your fears. Mine. It would be a mistake to get involved."

"A big mistake," she agreed, yet she knew they were already involved.

She felt him incline his head and sensed his mouth was only inches from hers. The flashlight forgotten, she wrapped her arms around his back.

It was then that she felt the light slip.

Desperately she grabbed for it, but it was too late. It hit Jason's boot with a soft thud, then the floor.

"Oh, no," she cried, pulling back.

Jason heard the anxiety in her voice and released his hold on her. Val could say what she liked about trust, but she was in a panic.

He heard her drop to her knees. "It should be right around here. Whatever you do, don't step on it or kick it with your foot."

The slap of her palm on the floor gave him a better idea of where she was. He knelt carefully, then also began looking for the flashlight.

He found it first and tried the switch. The moment the light came on, he heard her sigh. Shifting the beam in her direction, he caught her settling into a sitting position near the wall. She looked his way and smiled faintly. "Maybe you'd better hold on to that one."

Her expression was a mixture of tension and relief, and he began to realize just how frightened she'd been, and that it wasn't because of him.

"You *are* afraid of the dark, aren't you?"

"Yes." She sighed again and patted a spot next to her. "Childish, isn't it? Come sit down. Give me a minute to recoup. Being with you is like riding a roller coaster."

He'd agree, though with her he felt more like a puppet on a string. "Maybe we'd better just forget this project."

"No," she said quickly. "We just need to remember why we're here. No more talk about trust. No more—"

She didn't finish, but he understood. Frustrated, he leaned back against the wall. "I take it we're back to hands off?"

She touched his hand. "Not that drastic, maybe, but I think we should stick to business. Don't you?"

Did he? He no longer knew what he should or should not do. Frustrated, he exhaled heavily. "I suppose."

For a minute she said nothing, then she asked, "How long were you married?"

"Five years."

"Do you miss your wife?"

Bud had asked him the same question. He hadn't answered Bud. He did answer Val. "Sometimes."

"Do you want to talk about her?"

"No."

A wall of silence fell between them. He knew he'd placed it there. He'd asked her to trust him. The question was, did he trust her? Could he?

He surprised himself when he began to speak. "Karen was a very special person. Caring. Loving. She was a breath of reality in a world of make-believe."

"It must have hurt when she told you she'd had an affair."

Jason glanced her way, and Val wished she'd kept

quiet. Yet she'd learned through therapy that talking about feelings helped.

"I was jealous as hell," he confessed. "Even though she said it had been a mistake and was over, I couldn't believe she'd do such a thing to me. I was too hurt to realize it was my fault, that I'd been away too long, had left her when she needed me."

"Do you know who the guy was?"

"No. Karen said she didn't want me to know, that it would be better that way." He scoffed. "It wasn't. That was one more reason I had to get away from L.A., Hollywood, the people we knew. Every man I saw, I wondered if he was the one."

"Do you think . . ." Val hesitated, then asked, "Do you think he killed her?"

"It's a possibility, but I don't know how."

"You never told the police about this other man?"

He laughed at the idea. "Val, I was in shock after walking into our living room and finding Karen lying on the floor, but I wasn't brain-dead. When I saw how that gun was rigged, I knew I'd be accused."

"Because you do special effects?"

"Yes."

"But if you'd told them there was another man, they would have had another suspect."

"After what happened to my brother? You know about that, don't you?"

"What I read in the papers." Two years before his wife's death a car crash had claimed Jason's brother's life. Val still remembered the headline she'd read on one of the tabloids while waiting to buy groceries. BROTHER OF FX GENIUS COMES BACK FROM THE DEAD TO TELL MOTHER ALL.

She'd bought that paper and read the article, which had suggested that Jason had had something to do with his brother's death. Even some of the more respectable papers had hinted at that.

"Wasn't your brother's death ruled an accident caused by defective brakes?"

"It was my car. And that morning I had threatened to kill him."

"But did you mean that threat? From what I read, you two were arguing over your wife and you told your brother to stay away from her."

"Or I would kill him," Jason finished. "I was jealous. I thought he was making a pass at her."

"Was he?"

A shrug was the only answer she got.

"Couldn't it have been you driving that car just as easily as your brother?"

"You sound like a lawyer now." Again he shrugged. "Okay. Yes, it could have been me driving that car. Except it wasn't. You want another opinion? Ask my mother. She thinks I killed Rob. She hasn't spoken to me since that day."

"That doesn't mean she's right." Val knew from experience that some people found it easier to blame others than to accept the truth.

"And it doesn't mean I didn't do it," Jason said, and rose to his feet. "See this scar?" He touched the jagged white line above his left eye. "That's where Rob's fraternity ring cut me. I remember that fight every time I look into the mirror, remember threatening to kill him. Maybe I wasn't thinking too straight that afternoon when I worked on my car . . . or maybe I was thinking very straight. I was the one who insisted Rob take my car that night. I knew how fast he always drove."

A shiver of fear ran down Val's spine, and she scrambled to her feet, facing him. "Don't talk like that, Jason. What do you want to do, scare me again?"

"Maybe you should be scared, Valerie. Maybe you need to think twice about asking me to work on this house."

She had thought twice. Three times and more. Each time she'd come to the same conclusion. They needed him.

Putting her hand over his, she pointed the flashlight he held toward the room across the hall. "In there," she said, hoping he couldn't detect the slight quaver in her voice, "we've created a maze using sheets hung from the ceiling." A little more pressure directed the beam of light toward the ceiling as they walked toward the room. "You can see the wires. We hang the sheets from the wires and tack the bottoms of them to the floor to keep the little kids from crawling under."

She felt his gaze on her, measuring her and gauging her sincerity. She didn't look him in the eyes, knowing how intimidating his dark gaze could be, but kept her focus on the room. Finally he, too, looked that way. "Just a maze?" he asked.

"With threads hanging down, so it feels like those cobwebs in the passageway. And, of course the lighting is minimal, little more than what we have now, and we play spooky music, with sound effects."

Growing more confident, she guided him to the next room. There she pointed out a coffin sitting in one corner. "A funeral parlor down in Grass Valley donated it to us. We have someone dressed like Dracula lie in there and sit up every so often. That's usually good for a scream or two. And down here is our witches' room." She led the way. "Last year we had three. Our witches offer apples to each person who walks by. A few people take them, but most refuse."

Val described each idea they'd used in the last few years. She knew none were unusual. Certainly nothing to entice large crowds to drive long distances and pay money. Nothing Jason couldn't do better.

They went down the stairs, and she stopped at the first room, using a key to open the door. "Here's where, after Sheriff Maxwell nearly fell through, we had to pull up some of the flooring. We keep the room locked just in case someone breaks in. We don't want anyone falling through the hole and suing us."

Jason directed the light into the small room. About a third of the way in part of the floor was missing. He could see the floor joists spanning an opening about five feet square. "The cellar's under here?"

"Yes. The trapdoor that gets you to it is in the next room."

Stepping into the room, Jason walked over to the missing section of flooring.

"Don't get too close," she warned, following him. "We're working on getting one of the lumberyards to donate some lumber, but everything seems to take so long."

"Don't be in a rush to fix this. It may be better that the floor is missing." Standing at the edge, he directed his light down to the cellar below. "Actually this is great. Just what I'd need. I—"

He turned to his left just as she walked up beside

him on his right. His right elbow touched her, nothing more. A tap on the back.

If she hadn't been so close to the edge, she would have been fine, could have caught her balance. As it was, all she caught was air.

Jason spun around and grabbed for her, crying out her name. He nearly lost his own balance, and did lose his grip on the flashlight. It plummeted downward after Val, rotating as it fell. He heard the dull thud of Val's body hitting hard dirt moments before the flashlight clinked against a rock. Immediately it went out.

"Valerie!" Jason shouted into the darkness.

There was no answer.

Fear coursing through him, he dropped to his knees and groped in the blackness for a floor joist. Finding one, he swung himself down until he was hanging above the cellar floor. He could hear Val gasping for breath and guessed where she lay. Hoping he would clear her, he released his hold and let himself drop. The jolt of impact traveled up through his legs.

His first impulse was to gather her into his arms, just as he'd gathered Karen's body when he'd found her. To hold Val close. Vanquish the terror.

Anger and fear raged within him. It wasn't fair, not again.

He managed to remember the first aid training he'd had and quell the impulse to grab her. Cautiously he reached out and touched her. "Don't move. I'll get help. Where do you hurt?"

Her breathing was ragged and coming in shallow gasps. Beneath his hand he felt her move. "I'm—okay— I think," she managed. "Wind—"

She didn't finish, and he ran his hand up her coat

sleeve until he found her neck. The rapid beat of her pulse frightened him. "Don't talk. Just lie still."

Again she ignored him, moving and rolling toward him, flexing her arms and rotating her shoulders. Each breath she sucked in sounded less labored, more rhythmic. He couldn't say the same for his heart rate.

She moved one leg, then the other.

He was also checking, sliding his hands over her body, wishing she weren't so bundled up, yet certain it was her layers of clothing that had buffeted her fall. "Anything broken?"

"I don't think so."

"I didn't push you." She had to believe that. "I didn't realize you were there."

She caught his hand, her fingers feeling so small and slender. "I know you didn't."

"I turned . . . you were . . ." He couldn't explain what had happened.

"I'm fine, really," she insisted, more conviction to her words.

She started to rise, but he stopped her. "Take a minute," he said, then chuckled. "So I can catch my breath."

"You all right?"

Her concern for him seemed ironic. Here he could have killed her, and she was worried about him. "I'm fine. It's you who could have broken your neck."

"But I didn't."

He drew her close, cradling her against his chest, and Val pressed her cheek to the smooth leather of his jacket. His breathing seemed normal, but not his heart rate. Touched by his concern, she snuggled closer. All around her was darkness, yet she wasn't afraid. Jason was a man who would protect her, chase the bogeymen away. "I've got to remember not to come up beside you near any cliffs."

He didn't laugh.

"Jason, forget it even happened."

"Forget?" He did make a sound that resembled a laugh, though it held no mirth. "Why is it accidents always happen around me?"

"Who knows?"

"Maybe I forget too much." He took in a deep breath. "Val, do you think a man can do something and not remember that he's done it?"

"Like?"

He hesitated a moment, then said, "Like rig a gun in a wall safe or tamper with a brake line?"

She didn't answer. What he was suggesting was insane.

"My mother says I can block it out if I want," he went on, "but that she knows the truth. According to her, I'm a bad seed. The Devil's child."

"And what do you think?"

"I didn't believe her at first, but then when Karen was killed—"

His arm tightened around her. "How do I know I'm not some sort of Jekyll and Hyde? That I don't black out or something when I get jealous? Perhaps, in a fit of rage, I did tamper with those brakes and rig that gun in the safe."

The thought was too frightening. Val tried to push it aside with clear logic. "Were your prints on the gun?"

"No, there were no prints."

"Do you think 'in a fit of rage' you'd make sure there were none?"

"Maybe not, but I did call Karen that morning and ask her to check if her passport was in the safe and was up-to-date."

"Why?"

"The reason I told the police and the jury was I was going to take her back to England with me for the finish work that needed to be done on the movie."

"And was that the reason?"

She heard his frustrated sigh. "That's the question, isn't it?"

Val's thoughts were in a jumble. Could there be a dark side to Jason, one he wasn't in control of or even aware of?

She'd loved and lived with a man who'd beat her. That had been bad enough. To get involved with a man who might kill her and never know it was insane.

It didn't make sense.

"People don't just do things like that once in a while," she said. "What about your childhood? Were you ever out of control then?"

"My parents called me a hellion. I was always into things, tearing everything apart to see how it worked. When I was in high school, I blew up a toilet in the boys' bathroom. I told the principal I wanted to see if what I'd learned in chemistry was true. Maybe it was the monster in me trying to get out. Maybe every scary creature I create is the monster."

"Maybe we all have monsters within us," she suggested. "What you're saying doesn't sound abnormal. You're a creative person. That's why you're in special effects. What about your brother? Didn't he get into trouble once in a while?"

Jason's laugh was harsh. "Rob? According to my mother, he was the perfect son. Always behaved himself, did well in school, didn't get suspended for blowing up toilets, and went on to college."

"Parents see what they want to see." She knew that firsthand. "Your brother wasn't perfect. Don't forget, he made a pass at your wife."

"What he did was console her when she needed a shoulder to lean on. But, of course, I overreacted." Jason sighed. "She should have married him, or someone like him. Karen needed a man who would be home every night, who would spend more time with her than with robots and miniatures. Someone normal."

"Normal can be dull." And Val would never call Jason dull. Exciting. Scary. Sexy. But never dull. "I'm sure your wife knew what she was getting into when she married you."

"Does any woman know what she's getting into when she marries a man?"

He was right, of course, Val thought. She certainly hadn't known. "Probably not. Nevertheless, your wife had to have been aware of what your work involved, of how much time was involved."

"Usually she didn't complain. Maybe things would have turned out differently if she had complained. Then Rob wouldn't have had to console her. And if I'd realized how much it really bothered her when she learned she could never have children, maybe I would have insisted she come to England with me. Actually I never should have gone."

Val heard the remorse in his voice, the lingering love for a woman who had died tragically three years earlier.

"I don't think you did it," she said positively. It just didn't seem possible.

"Your opinion."

"And a jury's."

"And a jury's," he repeated.

There was no conviction to his words, only pain. She touched his face. The stubble of a day's growth of beard was rough against her palm. Lightly she stroked his jaw. "You're no killer."

"I could have killed you tonight."

"That was as much my fault as yours. Here I tell you not to get too close to the edge, and I go and do it myself. My falling was an accident."

"Accidents seem to happen when I'm around." He placed a hand over hers, moving her fingertips to his lips. He kissed them. "I don't want anything to happen to you."

It was too late, she thought. Things had been happening since the day she'd walked into his house, feelings she couldn't control. Just the touch of his lips was like dynamite, sparking an explosion to the toes of her shoes.

She melted against him, tilting her head so he found her mouth. His lips played over hers, the sensations a thousand times more exhilarating, the danger more real than a fall. Emotionally she was in shock, off balance and reeling. She clung to him, holding on for stability.

He lay back on the ground, bringing her with him. From deep within came her groan of submission.

Immediately he drew his head back. "Did I hurt you?"

"No," she assured him, not wanting him to stop. What they were doing was a dream, unreal and magical.

In the darkness that surrounded them, only feelings mattered, the need and the satisfaction.

His mouth found hers again, and she responded with a fervor born of relief. This was no monster holding her. This was a man, strong and caring. A man torn with doubts and burning with desire.

A man she could love.

The thought frightened her. For three years she'd protected herself from hurt by sealing off her heart. On her few dates, she gave her kisses sparingly. Her emotions were always moderated and controlled. With Jason, she was willingly treading dangerous ground, teetering on the edge of sanity.

She welcomed his marauding tongue and imagined knowing him in a more intimate way. How easy it would be, in the cloak of darkness, to follow their passions, to give heed to the rising ache deep within her.

As if reading her mind, he unbuttoned her coat and pushed it open. His hands spanned her waist, pulling her tighter against him. She felt his need and knew the temptation was not hers alone.

Close to her ear, he spoke her name, the sound ragged and breathless and filled with promise. Almost simultaneously, from somewhere above, Val heard a woman call her name.

Jason drew his head back. Val held her breath and tried to hear over the pounding of her heart. The members of WIN had circulated the story of ghosts to promote their haunted house, but she'd never considered it a possibility. Could she have been wrong?

"Val?"

Again the sound drifted down from above, clearly a woman's voice and definitely closer. It was no ghost, Val realized, but Debbie. Up above, the beam of a flashlight pierced the darkness.

"Are you in here?" Debbie called.

"Down here," Jason yelled back, rising to his feet. "Watch the hole in the floor."

SIX

By the time Debbie flashed her light down through the opening in the floor, Val was also on her feet, dusting the dirt from her coat and slacks and wondering how she could dust away what she'd nearly done. She hoped the dim lighting would mute the coloring in her cheeks. Embarrassment mingled with lingering excitement.

"What are you doing down there?" Debbie asked, spotlighting Val first, then Jason.

Making love, Val thought. The giddy realization turned her gaze to Jason. He was watching her, his guarded expression revealing none of the passion they'd just shared. She looked back at Debbie. "I fell," she said. "Jason came down to make sure I was all right."

"Fell?" Debbie brought the light back to her. "Are you all right?"

"Fine."

"You could have been killed."

"Now you sound like Jason. It was an accident."

"Why were you prowling around this house in the dark?" Debbie asked.

"Actually there's a flashlight down here some-where," Jason said, finally speaking up. "It also fell."

Debbie scanned the floor of the cellar with her light, illuminating the papier-mâché tombstones they'd stored down there, along with the boxes of supplies they carried over from year to year. Both Jason's hat and his flashlight were about ten feet from where Val stood. Surprisingly, when Jason tried the light, it worked.

"I'll get the trapdoor," Debbie said, and stepped back from the hole in the floor.

The moment she was gone, Jason came to Val's side. "You all right?" he asked quietly.

She knew he wasn't asking about her physical well-being, and she wasn't sure how to answer. Only minutes before, she'd been aroused—so quickly, so easily—almost to the point of no return. If Debbie hadn't arrived, chances were she and Jason would be making love at this very minute.

"I'm a little shaken," she admitted.

"Things got out of hand."

It wasn't the phrase she'd use, but she understood his meaning. "Probably a good thing Debbie showed up."

"Probably."

That he spoke without conviction warmed her. She touched the flashlight in his hand. "I'm surprised that works."

"Tonight's been full of surprises."

And revelations, she would add. They needed to talk, but there was no time before Debbie lifted the trapdoor and shone her light on the steps fifteen feet away. "I was on my way back from dropping a coffee cake off for Eva Reece," she said, crouching down to look at them. "When I saw your cars, I thought I'd stop. Why are you here?"

"We've been checking out the house," Val answered. "Wait until you see what Jason found."

Debbie's expression, when Jason showed her the secret panel in the downstairs closet, was one of amazement. She would not, however, go inside the passageway, nor would she even stand close to Jason.

All three of them left soon after that. Jason told Val he'd be in touch, and she expected a call that night. It didn't happen.

Thursday she worked at the clinic in Grass Valley, but was back by seven. All evening she waited for the phone to ring. The only call she received was from her mother. Friday she was at her office in Slaterville. Every time the outside door opened or Ginger greeted someone, Val paused and listened. It was never Jason. That night she cursed her answering machine for having no messages, and every time the phone rang, her stomach twisted uncomfortably. Considering how close she and Jason had come to making love on the floor of the cellar, she'd expected some sort of contact.

On Sunday she nearly called him. At seven P.M. she actually had her hand on the phone before she swore at herself and made brownies instead. "Men!" she grumbled, plopping down on the sofa and snapping on the television as she waited for the brownies to bake. "Who needs them?"

She was fifteen minutes into a show when the oven timer went off. She went to the kitchen, pulled out the pan, and set it on the stovetop to cool. As she turned toward her kitchen window she saw Jason pull into her driveway.

Just the sight of him made her heart leap. She dashed to her bedroom, where she checked her appearance and groaned. Her mother always used to chide her about getting half the ingredients on herself whenever she cooked. This night was no exception. Her blue and gold UC Berkeley sweatshirt and sweatpants were smudged with flour and chocolate. Floppy slippers covered her feet, and she couldn't remember the last time that day she'd put on lipstick or combed her hair. Taking the most important first, she ran her fingers through her hair, taming the wildest of her curls. Before she got any further, Jason was knocking on her door.

"Leave it to a man," she muttered, and decided he would get what he got. Thursday, Friday, and Saturday she'd made certain she looked her best, just in case he might stop by. Tonight she'd given up on him, and here he was.

She opened the door.

"Hi," she said coolly, her smile forced. "What a surprise."

His gaze slowly traveled down over her outfit to her slippers, then he looked back at her face and grinned. "I suppose I should have called first."

"If you were trying to discover the real me, you've got her."

Jason could tell Val was embarrassed and kicked himself for not phoning. He remembered how Karen had hated company dropping by unexpectedly. "A woman likes to look her best," she'd always said. He'd thought she looked great all of the time and couldn't understand her fuss. And right now he thought Val looked great—casual, relaxed. Sexy.

He liked the way her sweatshirt sagged and bagged, resting softly on the curves of her breasts. And the spot of chocolate right where the letter *U* covered her right breast was tempting. He'd always loved chocolate.

"Baking?" he asked.

"Brownies," she said, glancing back toward her kitchen. "I just pulled them out of the oven. Come on in. Do you like brownies?"

"Do producers like blockbusters?" he asked, then chuckled. "Old work joke. I love brownies."

He took off his hat and jacket, hanging them on a hook by the door, and followed her into the kitchen. He was carrying a notebook. "I've been working on some ideas. I thought if you had time tonight, I'd run them by you."

"Sure, why not."

She sounded a little cool, and she barely looked his way as she got out two plates and forks. He had a feeling he knew why.

He should have called. Not just tonight, but before. He should have apologized for what happened in that cellar—for what happened every time he was around her. He was in no position to get involved with her, not with the shadow of Karen's murder still hanging over his head and not as long as he had doubts about his innocence.

He should have called, but somehow he hadn't been able to.

Simply hearing Val's voice did things to him. Even the thought of her made him want the impossible. So he'd fought thinking about her, concentrating instead on the task she'd given him. Setting his imagination free, he'd played with possibilities for the haunted house, and the ideas had flowed.

The only problem was, working on the haunted house hadn't completely erased thoughts of Val. Each room he'd considered brought back memories of what she'd said that night, memories of how she'd looked and smelled . . . and felt.

Even now he wondered if he hadn't worked as fast as he had simply so he could see her again. He'd come that night because he couldn't stay away any longer.

"Would you like some coffee?" she asked politely.

"Sounds good."

He watched her start the coffeemaker and dish out the brownies. They exchanged comments about the recent warmer weather and how high the Yuba River was from the spring melt. He might have been talking to a stranger, and in a way, he realized, he was. He knew so little about Valerie Wiggins.

"Let's take these into the living room," she said, handing him his plate with a brownie.

She snapped off the television and cleared a work area on her coffee table. He sat on the sofa, placing his notebook on the center of the table and his plate to the side. She tossed another log on the fire in her fireplace, then positioned herself on the opposite end of the sofa, a good two feet away from him. Her body language was saying "don't touch." He obeyed and attacked his brownie instead.

"I'm glad you've been working on ideas," she said, picking at her own brownie. "It must have kept you very busy."

"Very," he agreed, brushing crumbs from his mouth.

"And will our haunted house outshine all others?"

"Guaranteed." He put down his fork, pulled out his glasses, slipped them on, and opened his notebook. "I made up what's called a storyboard. We do them for movies. What I'm going to do is take you from the moment you drive up to the house until you leave."

He scooted closer so she could see the sketches he'd made. His knee brushed hers, and he could feel her tense, but she didn't move away. His first drawing was of the outside of the house.

"How long did you say you usually have your haunted house open?" he asked. "A week before Halloween? Two weeks?"

"Two," she answered, frowning as she puzzled over his sketch.

"Leaving your house vacant fifty weeks of the year." He glanced at her, then wished he hadn't. A few crumbs lingered on her lips, and he had a sudden urge to lean over and kiss them away, to run his fingers through her mocha-brown curls and hold her close. Clenching his hands, he looked back at the sketch. "How long's the tourist season up here?"

"Late May through early September, usually. We get a few visitors in town before and after, but the bulk come during those months. You're suggesting . . . ?"

"That your group keep this house open longer than two weeks, at least as long as the tourist season. That you expand your ideas and incorporate the history of the house. I've gone back a couple of times since Wednesday night. I used the secret passageway to get in. What I was thinking . . ."

Val listened to his ideas and looked at the sketches he turned over, yet a part of her mind wandered off on its own tangent. Sitting so close to Jason was having a now familiar effect on her. Breathing in his clean, woodsy scent, she wondered if he was wearing a cologne or an aftershave. He'd shaved before coming over. She could tell by the smoothness of his chin.

As slovenly as she looked, he was perfectly dressed. With his glasses on and the touch of gray in his hair, he looked distinguished; and his leather boots, designer jeans, and blue wool sweater all screamed quality. None of his clothing was covered with flour or chocolate. Only his hair had a slightly unruly look, mussed from his hat, one lock falling sexily down over his forehead. She quelled an urge to push it back into place.

"What do you think?" he asked, and she pulled her gaze away from his hair. Evidently he'd asked a question.

"I—ah." She didn't know what to say. "I'm not sure."

"I know it's quite a departure from what you've been doing, but I think it would have a broad appeal and provide you with a steady flow of visitors.

"What you'd be offering," he went on, "would be a glimpse of the past packaged in the future: part visual and part interactive. Holograms are always fascinating, and with a few animated models here and there, some realistic sound effects, I think you'd have people driving for miles to see your haunted house."

"A few animated models? *Holograms?*" She stared at him in disbelief. "Jason, your friend Bud said it clearly enough. We don't have that kind of money. You're working with a volunteer organization functioning on a limited budget, not a movie studio."

"You hold pledge drives, don't you?" he asked seriously. "Take donations?"

"Yes, but we don't raise the kind of money it would take to do what you're proposing. And what we do raise, we need to run the safe house."

He reached over and squeezed her knee. "Forget about the money for now. What do you think of the idea?"

"What do I think?" She stared at him. His hand on her knee had every nerve in her body tingling. Thinking was totally impossible. In the kitchen, the coffee machine gave its final gurgle. She stood. "I think I'll get our coffee."

Once away from him and out of his sight, she leaned against her kitchen counter and closed her eyes. What was she going to do? She'd asked for his help, and he'd come up with an idea that was entirely impossible. Simply being in the same room with him was impossible. She was acting like a love-starved idiot. She wasn't prepared to deal with this, with him.

Her hand was shaking as she poured the two coffees. "Cream or sugar?" she called into the living room.

"Black," he yelled back.

She took two deep breaths and tried to calm her nerves. She would simply have to tell him that they couldn't do what he was suggesting. He'd probably be upset after spending as much time as he evidently had working on the project, but his anger might help. It would put everything back into perspective for her. She'd been a fool to think a Hollywood special effects man would understand the needs of a small-town volunteer group. Just as she'd been a fool to think a few kisses and a little groping in a dark cellar meant anything. It was time to get such crazy thoughts out of her mind.

The decision made, she picked up the two mugs of coffee and walked back into the living room. He was still seated on the sofa, studying his sketches. Leaning forward, she started to put his mug of coffee down on the table.

He moved at the same time, lifting his arm. His hand hit hers, the impact loosening her grip. The mug slipped and fell.

She heard his yelp of pain and watched him jump to his feet. When his raised hand came down, she reacted automatically. Dropping the other mug, she fell to her knees, her arms raised to protect her head and face.

She heard him swear and say her name. Her eyes squeezed closed, she waited for the first blow. Memories of other blows still so vivid, memories of pain and fear, exploded in her mind. She was sobbing when she realized the hands touching her were not hurting but giving comfort, that the arms around her were not going to harm her. Jason was on his knees in front of her, rocking her, soothing her with the calming murmur of his voice. "Don't cry," he said over and over. "It's all right."

Embarrassment replaced fear, and slowly she controlled the tears. A sob turned into a hiccup. She held her breath, gradually let it out, then looked at him. The lower half of his sweater and the front of his jeans were soaked with spilled coffee. No wonder the man had yelled and jumped.

The reality of what she'd done shook her. "How badly are you burned? Let me get some ice."

She started to stand, but he stopped her, a steellike

grip on her wrist keeping her on her knees and close. "I don't need any ice," he said firmly. "What I need is to understand what just happened, what you were thinking."

"I . . ." She couldn't answer and looked away, avoiding the intensity of his dark, questioning gaze.

"Are you *that* afraid of me?"

"Not of you," she confessed, glancing back. "It was just an automatic reaction."

"Automatic?" he repeated, and shook his head. "Come here." Settling against the sofa and stretching out his long legs, he brought her with him, snuggling her close to his side. His glasses came off and he tossed them onto the coffee table. "I don't hit women, Val. In fact, I don't usually hit men."

"I never thought you did." She looked down at the carpeting. His gaze was too inquiring, the truth too painful. The area around them was as soaked as his clothing, and a few feet away the two mugs she'd held lay on their sides, empty.

Jason rubbed a hand up and down the sleeve of her sweatshirt, his touch a soothing balm. "Tell me about it," he said gently. "What you were thinking a few minutes ago?"

"What's there to tell?" Actions spoke louder than words. "I thought you were going to hit me."

"Why?"

"Why?" Looking at him, she realized he didn't understand. "Because if I'd spilled that coffee on Mike, he wouldn't have just let loose with a few swear words."

"You're still that conditioned? How long has it been since he last hit you? Ten years?"

She hated to admit the truth, and her answer was barely audible. "Three."

"Three? But I thought—"

She could understand his confusion. She hadn't understood herself. "Three years ago Mike showed up at my apartment in Sacramento, said he'd changed and that he still loved me."

"So you took him back?"

Again she looked down at the carpet. "Don't ask me why; I really don't know. I guess it's his charisma. That's what drew me to him in the first place. And I thought he had changed." That she'd changed.

"But he hadn't?"

She sighed. "Everything was fine for a month. We did things together, got to know each other again. He was charming and fun. In fact, we were talking about getting remarried. And then, one day, he ran into an old buddy of his and they went out for a few drinks. Mike didn't get home until late. I got on his case about it, and he hit me. The next day he was all apologetic and said it was because he'd been drinking and he'd never do it again. And like an idiot, I once again forgave him.

"Here I'd gone through all this therapy, had a degree in optometry, and thought I had my act together. I don't know what it is about Mike. I'm not like that with other men. Just the hint of abuse—verbal or physical—and I'm through with them. But with Mike . . ."

Again she sighed. "Everything was fine for another two weeks. Then one day I had a job interview. An important one. I came home all excited. I'd been offered a position in a major eye-care center in Sacramento. It was just what I'd wanted. What I didn't know was Mike had lost his job that day. The moment I walked through the door, I knew things weren't right. I ended up in the emergency room that night." She looked at Jason. "But what was worse, when he asked me to forgive him, I almost did. I knew then that I had to get away from him. Far, far away."

"So you came up here."

She nodded. "I turned down the job offer with that eye company, moved up here, and hoped he'd never find me."

"And where is this ex-husband of yours now?" Jason asked, half considering a visit to the man.

"Prison. My mother's kept track of him. Two months after he put me in the hospital, Mike punched a cop who'd picked him up for drunk driving."

"All-around nice guy."

"A real winner. Considering his past record, they threw the book at him."

"And when he gets out . . . then what happens?"

"As far as I know, he doesn't know where I'm living."

"But if he shows up?"

"I'll tell him to keep on going, and if he doesn't, I'll call Sheriff Maxwell or one of his deputies and have them keep Mike away from me."

"Are you still in love with him?"

"No."

She said it firmly, but Jason wondered.

"Afraid of him?"

She hesitated, then shook her head. "I don't think he'd do anything."

"And what about me?"

"You?" She looked confused.

"Are you going to be cringing every time I move my arms?"

The warmth was back in her smile. "No."

There was one way to find out, Jason decided. Moving quickly, he changed their positions, taking her down flat on her back on the wet carpet and pinning her hands by her sides. Straddling her, he watched her face, looking for signs of fear. What he saw in her eyes was surprise, then a flicker of passion. Immediately his body reacted.

He had his answer. He also had a problem. Groaning, he released her. He pushed himself to his feet and walked over to her fireplace.

He was aware of her movements behind him, of her getting up and coming near. She said nothing, but touched his sweater, lifting it away from his skin before raising it. He was vaguely cognizant of the heat from the fire reaching his skin and some pain, but it was nothing compared to the ache deep within.

Val was aware of far more. The muscles of Jason's abdomen were flat and hard, and a thatch of dark hairs narrowed down from his chest to disappear beneath the waist of his jeans. Wet from the coffee, his denims clung to his hips, outlining a prominent bulge. For a moment she stared, then pulled her gaze back to his face. "Your skin's red," she said, her voice shaky.

"I'll live."

He was staring at her bare mantel, his hands clenching the cheap marble. She lowered his sweater back into place, then touched his arm. "Jason, what's wrong?"

He turned to face her, his expression dark and brooding. "Everything's wrong, that's what. I shouldn't be here, shouldn't be around you. I have my own demons. Now I'm stirring up yours."

"Maybe they need to be stirred up. Faced."

"Maybe there are other things that shouldn't be stirred up, things better left . . . untouched."

He could be right, she mused. They were swimming in dangerous waters, and like the torrential Yuba in the springtime, unchecked emotions could sweep them away. On the other hand, to avoid the danger meant missing out on the thrill. Safety did not guarantee happiness. "A little stirring keeps life interesting."

"I shouldn't have come tonight. The first time I saw you, I knew you were trouble."

She smiled, remembering his reaction to her that first meeting. "All you did was scowl at me."

"And wonder how it would feel to touch your hair." He reached out and touched her curls, snaking his fingers into their tangles. "To touch you. Val . . ."

He whispered her name, the sound as elusive as the wind whispering through the tips of the pines. The slightest pressure of his fingers against her scalp brought her closer, and she tilted her head so that she was gazing directly into his eyes. What she saw was temptation and promise.

"I wanted you then," he said huskily. "And I want you now."

SEVEN

"And I want you," Val said, knowing it was the truth. Ever since the night they'd been together in the haunted house, she'd felt incomplete and unfulfilled.

Jason studied her face, his expression guarded. "You're sure?"

She was sure that the slightest touch of his hand put her whole world out of focus, sure that she was no longer seeing anything straight, and sure that she didn't care. "Yes," she whispered.

She rose on her toes to meet his kiss. Suspended in time and space, she savored the feel of his lips, the give and take of his mouth. No corner was left untouched, no contour uncharted. He nibbled and nipped, then traced the line of his assault with the tip of his tongue. She matched him, giving as she received, believing she was his equal.

Then she parted her lips . . . and he invaded.

The first thrust of his tongue eliminated their equality, taking away her control. Deep inside, between her legs, an ache begged to be satisfied. She clung to his arms, a moan of desire betraying her ecstasy and agony.

He murmured something, she didn't know what, but she heard the satisfaction in his voice.

The moment his hands touched her waist, she sucked in a breath. His fingers were hot, drawing her closer. He pressed her hips against his, and there was no doubting his arousal. A shiver skittered down her spine, then spiraled through her body.

"Cold?" he asked.

"No," she said breathlessly. "Are you?"

"No." He nipped at her earlobe. "Anything but cold."

With the tip of his tongue and the warmth of his breath, he teased her, nibbling his way down her neck. Beneath the soft cotton of her sweatshirt, he slid his hands up to her ribs, his fingers resting just below her breasts. "Hmm," he murmured. "I never knew eye doctors felt this soft . . . or smelled this good."

He dropped his head lower, capturing a taut nipple through her sweatshirt and sucking it into his mouth. The moist, warm sensation held her captive, teasing her into wanting more.

He was smiling when he looked up. "You even taste good."

Slowly he lifted her sweatshirt, exposing her breasts. She hadn't worn a bra, and she waited, unsure what his reaction would be to her. Mike had considered her breasts too small, had even suggested implants. Once, if they'd had the money, she might have had it done. Now she was wiser.

She was what she was.

"Beautiful," Jason said, the look in his eyes echoing the word.

He pulled her sweatshirt off over her head, letting it drop to the floor. Again he glanced down at her, and again he lowered his head.

This time no cloth separated mouth from nipple, no cotton absorbed the moist warmth of him or muted the soft suckling of his lips. Like the sun in July, he heated her from the outside in, melting her.

He eased her to the carpeting, then continued his assault, dividing his time between her lips and her breasts, while his hands traveled lower. She held her breath when he dipped his fingers below the elastic waistline of her sweatpants. The tightening between her legs moistened her panties.

He slipped his hand lower, and the tip of one of his fingers grazed her most sensitive spot. She jerked involuntarily and, closing her eyes, groaned, absorbing all she could feel. Gently, provocatively, he caressed her, investigating the liquid warmth that awaited him, stroking her toward the edge of fulfillment, yet leaving her aching for him.

"Jason . . ." she begged, placing a hand on his arm.

He smiled knowingly and drew back, leaving her wanting what he'd taken away. Rolling to his side, he pulled off his sweater and kicked off his shoes. Every angle and plane of his profile was imprinted in her mind, along with the smile he cast her before pulling off his jeans.

She did glance down once, long enough to see the bulge beneath his pale blue briefs. He was as ready as she was. Then she looked back into eyes that seduced and promised so much to come.

As he drew her sweatpants down, she helped him, lifting her hips, then kicking off her slippers. Again she shivered, frightened by the emotions rushing through her. Giving herself to a man was not something she did lightly. Physical need alone had not brought her to this point.

"Scared?" Jason asked, getting a condom from his wallet.

"A little."

"So am I." Once again he stretched out beside her.

"You?"

"I may disappoint you."

She grinned at the possibility. "I don't think so."

"It's been a long while. I'm not going to last long."

"And I'm not keeping time."

"I may never get enough of you."

She didn't know what to say, but it didn't matter. He moved over her, his mouth covering hers, and words became inconsequential. Feelings took over. Anxiety turned to pleasure as his caresses renewed his acquaintance with her body.

She wasn't sure when her underwear went . . . or his. It didn't matter. She helped him slip on the condom, a need to touch him and be touched by him ruling her thoughts. Soon it was body against body—rubbing, stimulating. Entering.

She'd known only one other man besides Mike. They'd lived together for six months, then had gone their separate ways. She hadn't felt any loss at his parting and had soon forgotten him.

From the first day she'd met Jason, she'd known he wasn't a man she'd easily forget. What had drawn her to him, even before they met, she would never know, but the moment he entered her, she felt complete.

Jason kissed her and moved slowly within her, afraid of hurting her and afraid he wouldn't last. In the span of a lifetime three years wasn't long to be without a woman, but it was long enough to make him savor every moment and sensation. He wanted to bring Val the same pleasure she was bringing him, to carry her over the same threshold. Caught between giving and receiving, he watched her face, delighting in her sighs and groans, in the breathless way she tensed, in the way her eyes opened wide and then closed with delight.

They were one at this moment, united. Two halves of a whole, blending and contrasting. Theirs was a dance, a tango of love—dipping and twirling, the tempo increasing. Reality lost meaning for him, fears and doubts disappeared, wrapped in the moist warmth of ecstasy.

She cried out, but he knew it wasn't in pain. The rhythm of her body became explosive, the shock waves ricocheting through her to him, carrying him beyond control. He gasped his pleasure and knew nothing would ever be the same again.

Jason slowly became aware of the world around him, of Val's warm body curled next to his, of the crackling of the fire in the fireplace, of the nubby texture of the carpeting pressed against his side. Opening his eyes, he found Val watching him, her eyes a sultry blue and her hair a tousled swirl of chocolate curls. A satisfied smile curved her lips. He grinned back. "Hi."

"Hi," she returned.

"You okay?"

"I'm okay."

He wasn't sure he could say the same. "Do I dare ask if that was as good for you as it was for me?"

Her expression sobered, and he wondered if he'd misinterpreted her reaction. She looked seriously at him, then licked her lips before speaking. "Have you ever had something be so good it scared you?"

"Scared like you're afraid you made a mistake?"

She shook her head. "No. Like it's too good to last." Reaching up, she tenderly touched his face. "You know, that evening I came to your house, I thought I knew all about you. I'd read so much, heard so much. But the more I get to know you, the more I realize I really don't know that much about you."

"And what would you like to know?"

"Your likes. Dislikes."

"In twenty-five words or less, I suppose."

"You can take as many words as you want."

He brushed a curl back and nibbled on her earlobe. "I like touching you." He skimmed her side with his hand and felt an encouraging shiver run through her. "Getting you excited."

"You're distracting me," she said, half laughing. "Really, what do you like?"

He answered seriously. "Stretching the boundaries. Creating effects that awe people. A challenge." Nothing fascinated him more. "Your haunted house is going to be a challenge."

She grimaced. "Those drawings you showed me . . . Your ideas are great. The problem is . . ."

A log in the fireplace fell with a crackle, sparks rising up the chimney and reflecting in her eyes. In the flame-flecked blue he saw concern. "What's the problem?" he asked.

"You said not to worry, but I don't see how we can do the things you came up with. I never should have asked you to work on this, never should have wasted your time."

He touched a finger to her lips and shook his head. "You're not wasting my time. That's what I was doing before you showed up at my door. This will work."

"But your friend Bud said—"

"Forget what Bud said. Maybe I'll have to make a modification here and there and call in a few paybacks for favors, but we'll get everything we need. The problem with Bud is his imagination only goes so far. He's always had the big budgets; I've had to make do with little before. I'll find ways."

"You really think we can do it?"

Her question was so cautious, he exaggerated the possibilities. "I *know* we can. Your group is going to have the spookiest haunted house anywhere in the Sierras. People from as far away as Reno and San Francisco will be talking about it. They'll drive for hours to see the ghosts that disappear into walls, doors that breathe, and the miner who shoots at them."

"You make it sound so easy." She sighed, stretching out, her hip rubbing against his thigh.

A jolt of need rocketed through him, and when he spoke, his voice was gravelly thick. "It's not going to be easy. It's going to take a lot of hard work and cooperation."

"Well, you have my full cooperation."

As she rubbed against him again, he understood.

———————◆———————

It was just after three the next afternoon when Jason arrived at Val's house. As he walked up to her door a jay in a nearby cedar scolded. It seemed as if everyone were scolding him today—birds, Mrs. Andrews at the post office, Sheriff Maxwell.

Mrs. Andrews's scolding had been administered with affection. "I hear you're going to be helping Dr. Wiggins with that haunted house," she'd said when he'd picked up his mail. Maternally she'd wagged her finger his way. "Heard you were over at her place last night. Don't you be doing anything that might hurt that gal. We all like her."

Sheriff Maxwell's warning had been more to the point. "Any 'accidents' happening that involve Valerie Wiggins, and I'll personally give you a lesson in Slaterville justice," he'd said.

The sheriff's threat didn't bother Jason, but the man had made him think. Making love with Val had been a big mistake. Every time they kissed was a mistake. Accidents did happen to people he cared about.

Besides, he was in no position to get involved with a woman. What could he offer her? Most of his money had gone for lawyers or was tied up in the probate courts. Half the people he met thought he was guilty, the other half weren't sure.

Even he wasn't sure.

He'd made Val a promise the day he'd agreed to help with the haunted house. He'd told her she would be safe, that nothing would happen. He had to make certain he kept that promise.

She might not like what he was about to do, but in the long run she would thank him.

Val opened her front door before he reached her porch. She looked pretty and perky, her smile as warm as a sunny day. There was a glow about her, a radiance of happiness. Even her clothing reflected her mood, her jeans casual and her peach sweater soft and cheerful.

He stopped at the bottom of the steps and solemnly nodded his greeting. "Ready?"

Her smile grew hesitant, and he knew she'd expected more, a smile from him at the least. Probably a hug or a kiss.

Considering the number of times they'd made love the night before, it was reasonable. But she wouldn't be getting hugs or kisses from him. Not today or any time in the future.

"Let me get my coat," she said, and stepped back inside.

He walked by her side to his Jeep, not once touching her. She tried to make small talk, asked how his morning had gone and what he'd done. He kept his answers short and noncommittal. It wasn't until they were both in the Jeep that he turned toward her. "We need to talk."

"About . . . ?" Her smile was completely gone, her question hesitant.

"Last night." He faced the windshield, unable to look at her. "What we did was a mistake."

"A mistake?" she repeated.

"This is a small town. My Jeep was seen at your place last night. People are already talking."

"Let them."

She wasn't making it easy for him. What he needed

to do was make her hate him, turn the confusion he saw in her eyes to disdain. "Maybe it doesn't bother you," he said sharply, "but it does me. People are going to jump to conclusions about us, and then when I take up with someone else, they'll be throwing stones my way. I've got enough people ready to string me up. I don't need more. So what we started last night is over."

"But I thought—"

"What?" he snapped, glaring at her. "That I was in love with you? Sorry, honey. I'll admit that I'm physically attracted to you, that every time I'm around you, I get aroused. But what we're talking about is lust, nothing more. Making love with you was a challenge. You said hands off, and that made me want you."

"I was just a challenge?"

Her voice caught, and the pain in her eyes cut through him. Once again he had to look away. "That's about it."

She didn't say anything, but he could hear her draw in an unsteady breath and knew she was struggling for control. He waited a minute before glancing her way. "The question is, in light of what I've just said, do you still want me working on this haunted house of yours?"

Tears welled in her eyes and a slight tremble touched her lips. She stared at him for a moment, then looked out the side window. He forced himself not to reach out and console her. He knew what he felt for her was more than lust, and that making love with her had been more than a challenge. If it had been that simple, he wouldn't be afraid for her.

To take his feelings any further was too dangerous. Today he cared about her. Tomorrow . . . ?

The possibility of love—and of jealousy—had to be

avoided at all costs. Until he knew for certain that he'd had nothing to do with Rob's or Karen's deaths, he didn't dare give in to his desires.

In silence he waited for her decision.

Finally he heard her take in a deep breath and saw her head lift. Still not looking his way, she spoke. "I don't think our personal feelings should have anything to do with your working on the house. I came to you for your expertise. That's what I need."

"Good enough." He started the Jeep and headed down the hill. She'd accepted his terms. Now if he could just abide by them.

Val said nothing during the short drive. She couldn't. The tears were too close to the surface, and she didn't want to cry, not in front of him.

She should have expected this. He was Hollywood, the world of movies, jet set people, and the fast track. Maybe she'd been a challenge for a while, but she'd certainly given in easily enough. How long had she known him? Less than a month.

When was she going to stop being such a fool?

Last night had been a dream come true, but she'd acted on impulse when she should have been thinking. She'd made love with him because she'd thought there was something special between them, that it was more than chemistry or a physical need. Oh yes, she was a fool. She was falling in love with him, and he was already thinking of taking up with someone else.

She should have remembered that sex and love didn't always go together with men. Mike had said that often enough. She should have remembered to protect her heart.

Jason didn't say anything more, not until he pulled

into the gravel parking area next to the Clifford house, then he faced her. "You okay?"

"I'm fine," she lied. "Ready to get to work."

"Good. I brought some things for us so we could take notes." Leaning around to the back seat, he got two clipboards, pens, and paper. "Tonight we divide up duties."

He had his storyboard in hand when he stepped out of the Jeep. For a moment he looked around. A breeze whispered through the tops of the pines, flopping the rim of his hat up. He pull it back down, then looked at her. "Make a note to check on the lot next to this one. See if it's for sale. You probably have ample parking space, but if this catches on as I think it will, you might need more."

Numbly Val made a note to check who owned the adjacent lot.

Going through the gate in the weather-beaten picket fence and along the walkway, he glanced over the sparse lawn that remained beneath the trees. "You might as well dump those papier-mâché tombstones in the cellar."

"Why?" She was the one who'd bent the chicken wire to create the right shapes, had spent hours applying layers of newspaper and paste over the frames, and had painted them a stone gray before coming up with the funny sayings on each.

"Too amateurish looking," he said. "Plus the sayings are corny. 'Here lies Wanna B. Rich, caught jumping a claim.'" He shook his head. "How corny can you get?"

Amateurish! Corny! Biting her tongue, she wrote down his order. In less than ten minutes he'd rejected both her body and her creative talents.

"Tickets will be sold outside." He waved his hand toward an open space near the porch. "We'll need to build a booth. Groups going through the house should be kept down to two to six persons, spaced at least three minutes apart. They can wait out here on the porch."

"I suppose you'll want lounge chairs for them," she said sarcastically. He seemed to have forgotten they were working on a limited budget.

"A couple of chairs might be a good idea, but the others can stand." Jason walked the length of the porch and looked around the side of the house, then called back to her. "Besides lumber for a booth, we'll need boards to cover the windows. That will keep it dark inside, even during the day, and cut down on the possibility of vandalism."

Val quickly estimated the number of windows they would need to cover. It would take a lot of boards.

Slowly Jason came back to where she stood. His eyes were on the house, not her. That he'd torn her dreams to shreds didn't seem to matter to him. He was the planner now—the engineer, inventor, and dreamer.

"You'll need a liability release," he said. "You can't be too careful these days."

She would agree with that.

"And you should have something to build the mood. A prelude to what will be inside, a flyer that sets the tone." Stopping beside her, he glanced her way. "Do you have anyone in your group who could write up something like that?"

Earlier she might have said herself, but after his comments about her tombstone sayings, she passed. "Debbie was majoring in creative writing before she dropped out of college."

"Good. See what she can come up with." He waited for her to open the door with her key. Once inside, he went on. "The moment our paying public steps inside, they are going to become part of a drama."

In the light of day the house never seemed spooky to Val, merely old. She glanced into the room on their left. They'd forgotten to lock the door, and she remembered how, less than a week earlier, a more personal drama had been played out in that room and on the cellar floor below.

A flush of embarrassment colored her cheeks. She'd been used, and she'd willingly let it happen. He'd gotten what he wanted, and now he was all business. No accidental touches. No smiles. In fact, he barely looked at her.

A click brought her attention back to Jason. He was checking the light switch. "Have the electricity turned on this week," he said. "Everything will have to be re-wired. We'll keep the walkways well lit, but from below, not above, so everything will take on an eerie look."

"What about the floor in there?" she asked, pointing toward the hole she'd fallen through. "I don't want to be knocked into the cellar again." Knocked for a loop.

The twitch of a muscle in his jaw told her he was also remembering what had happened less than a week ago. That was the only sign he gave, though. "Once I get the cables and wiring in," he said, "we can close up that hole. Meanwhile, lock the door and keep it locked."

"Wiring and cables?" She walked over and closed the door, slipping her key into the lock.

"I've been thinking about what you said last night, about the cost. Maybe high-tech computer-driven animatronics are out of the question, but I can do a lot with hydraulics and a few simple electric motors and cams."

He pointed toward the closed door. "In there will be four miners playing cards around a table and a couple of ladies of the evening hanging over their shoulders. Their actions will be choreographed like a dance routine. When someone steps on a pressure bar we'll place under the carpeting out here"—he indicated a spot near their feet—"it will create an electrical connection that will start the sequence."

"And the cost?" Val still wasn't convinced that he understood their budget limitations.

"Not all that much. Automotive shops, junkyards, and secondhand stores will have a lot of the things I need. I've been rebuilding motors since I was twelve and repairing hydraulic pumps most of my life. What I come up with won't have the sophistication of a Disney World display, but it will tantalize your viewers."

They walked through the rest of the house, following the path Jason had mapped out on his storyboard. The first room would have the poker game. While the action was going on, a taped narration would be setting up the time period and relating the tales of Eldon Clifford's infamous poker games, including the story of the missing San Francisco politician. Finally a poker player, with his back to the viewers, would stand and accuse Clifford of cheating. In the second room the murder of Clifford would take place. And in the third room a woman dressed in black, supposedly Clifford's mistress, would relate how Clifford's ghost had been seen flitting through the house and was thought to be guarding the remains of the missing politician and perhaps a hidden cache of gold. The viewer's job was to find the skeleton and the gold.

From that point on, each room would have something to frighten or lure the searchers on. There would be paintings with moving eyes, doors that seemed to expand, and ghosts that disappeared through walls until, at last, near the end of the underground passageway a skeleton would be found, along with a map. Each map could then be turned in at the gift shop that would be in the shed and each searcher would receive a gold-plated coin imprinted with the haunted house's logo.

As they came to each room Val made notes. She also noted how Jason avoided standing near her or looking at her, how he would move away when she came up close, and how he kept their conversation strictly on the house.

At the stairs he pointed upward. "On the walls here, we'll install what look like candles in candleholders, except they'll move, and the holders will be models of human hands. Each light will be synchronized to come on and rotate as the party goes up the stairs, sort of pointing the way.

"Then, upstairs, Eldon Clifford's ghost will disappear through the wall into the first room, and when you walk into that room, reaching, grabbing arms and hands will come out of the walls. That, accompanied by the right moans and groans, should keep the group moving."

"You have a sick mind, Jason McLain," she said, imagining the scene. "And where do we find these arms and hands?"

He made a note on his own list. "I'll provide them."

"Maybe I *should* be afraid of you," she said, joking.

He didn't smile. "Maybe you should be."

His seriousness bothered her, and she quickly followed him up the stairs. "I was kidding."

He turned and faced her. "I'm not."

It was then that she understood why he was pushing her away.

Jason continued going through the rooms, describing how he would create each effect. Val wrote down what was needed, all the while trying to decide what she needed for her own special effects. First of all, an illusion of acceptance. Jason had to think she'd accepted his claim that all he felt for her was lust, that they had no future. It was the only way they might.

She should have understood from the beginning. He'd come to Slaterville to hide, but she'd tempted him out of his darkness. Now he was building a wall around himself. In order for her to penetrate it, he had to believe it was intact.

For a moment in his car she'd forgotten all she'd learned in the last ten and a half years. She'd once again allowed herself to be a victim, to accept the hurt. Her vision had become fuzzy, but she was in focus now. He liked a challenge. Well, so did she. What she needed were a few tricks, ways to make things appear different from what they really were.

On paper, Val's list was becoming longer and longer, and it didn't include any of the needs for the animated models or the holograms Jason thought he could get a friend to donate for the publicity. Simply getting everything set up and functioning by Halloween seemed an impossible task. They had just five months.

She gave herself the same deadline for getting Jason to acknowledge that what he felt for her was more than lust. Five months to get him to stop worrying about what he had done in the past and might do in the future.

Val prayed it would be long enough.

EIGHT

May was a month of change. The weather turned warmer, birds were nesting, and every member of WIN solicited donations for the haunted house. Jason gave each volunteer the list of items he needed and some ideas of where to look. After that, it was a matter of seek, find, and cajole.

Soon the cellar of the old Clifford house was filled with costumes, small electric motors, spools of wire, dress mannequins, and boxes of lightbulbs. They'd also received a large amount of money. Jason wasn't surprised; domestic violence was now a matter of national concern. Val, however, seemed amazed. "Maybe we should forget the haunted house and just go for the money," she said late one night.

Jason glanced up from the soldering job he was doing. Val had been in the kitchen, entering the most recent donations into the ledger she was keeping. Now she stood in the doorway to the first room, the "game room," as they'd dubbed it. All of the other workers had gone home.

As he'd predicted, she was the one who'd been chosen to work closely with him. What had surprised him was her acceptance of the job. Considering how he'd treated her, he'd expected her to refuse.

She tapped the closed ledger. "We're getting quite a healthy balance. I almost hate to turn around and spend the money on this house."

"And what about next year? And the next?" Jason asked. "Do you think you'll be able to muster this kind of response again? Would your volunteers be as aggressive if they didn't have this project?"

Just the slightest of sighs escaped her. "I suppose you're right." She motioned toward the jumble of parts on the floor. "But is this really going to work?"

"O ye of little faith." He chuckled, but understood her concern. He knew the wire structures lying on the floor around him looked nothing like gambling miners and bar girls. Without their parts put together and clothing to cover the wire framework, the objects were nothing more than cams and shafts, universal joints and electrical motors.

In his mind he saw everything assembled, with the latex heads and hands that the high school art teacher was working on attached. He could picture how the bodies would be dressed, the clothes covering the mechanical workings, and what each model would do once in place. He knew the chaos that occurred in the creation of all animated models. Val, like most moviegoers, went to *Star Wars* and *Jurassic Park* and saw only the final illusion.

"Think we'll have everything working by October?" she persisted.

"We don't have any choice, do we?" He went back

to soldering a small electrical motor into one miner's chest. "We'll make it."

The soft sound of her footsteps on the wood floor alerted him that she was walking over to him. He didn't look up but continued working. It was the only way he could keep himself from reaching out and touching her.

For a month now he'd forced himself to keep his hands off her, to ignore the desire to brush a cobweb from her hair or wipe a bit of dirt from her cheek. He knew it was best this way. It just wasn't easy.

"Mike was an absolute klutz when it came to repairing anything," she said, and Jason did glance up. Rarely did she speak about her ex-husband.

"My father was even worse," she went on. "If something broke, we either tossed it or called a repairman." She pointed toward the motor he was soldering. "What will that do?"

"See this?" He pointed at a circular metal disk with two pins sticking up at different distances from the center. "When a rod is connected to this pin here and to the arm, every time this cam goes around, the arm will move. This guy's going to be scratching his head as he looks at his cards. What was your father like?"

Jason could tell his question caught her off guard. For a moment he didn't think she would answer, then she shrugged. "Strict."

"Abusive?" he guessed.

" 'Abusive' is a general term. My father never physically abused me. I don't even remember him spanking me. What he did was mentally terrorize me . . . and my mother."

She smiled, but it didn't reach her eyes. "Have you ever been locked in a closet for two days?"

"Two days?"

"He said it was for my own good, that I deserved it for leaving lights on all through the house."

Jason remembered her fear of the dark that first night in this house. Now he understood. "That was pretty drastic punishment for leaving lights on."

"Not as drastic as when he shaved my head."

"Your father shaved your head?"

She nodded. "I'd used one of those hair preparations that's supposed to highlight your natural color. He didn't like it, said I looked like a punk, so he shaved me bald."

"How old were you?"

"Fourteen."

An age when a girl was extremely sensitive about how she looked. Jason's heart went out to Val. He could understand why she'd married so young. Mike would have been an escape.

Just her luck that she'd run to someone worse.

"How did you turn out so normal?"

"I didn't," she said, a weariness to her words and a sag to her shoulders. "You're looking at a grown woman who sleeps with a light on, who allowed herself to be physically abused, and who fell—"

She stopped abruptly, her gaze locked with his, then she shook her head and turned away. "I'm calling it a night. See you sometime tomorrow."

" 'Night," he said as he watched her leave.

It frightened him that he wanted to go after her, that he wanted to protect her and keep her from ever being hurt or humiliated again. He had to guard against those feelings, had to keep himself from caring.

For to care would put her in danger.

◆━━━━━━━━━━━━━◆

During the month of June the old wiring in the house was stripped away and new circuits were installed. Pressure sensors were put in place, then covered with new carpeting, and as soon as Jason knew where he wanted to run his cables and wires, the missing floor section in the game room was repaired. Val was surprised by how many places a person could find small electrical motors and how willing people were to donate them, but it was the hydraulic arms that Jason created that fascinated her. With the right lighting, people wouldn't notice that the arms were covered with acrylic and vinyl, not flesh, especially since they wouldn't be expecting bodiless hands to be grabbing for them.

By July most of the volunteers who'd been afraid of Jason initially were laughing at his subtle humor and cursing him for his attention to detail. Even Debbie began to relax around him, though she never would go into the secret passageway with him.

The only person he kept at arm's length was Val, but she knew he cared. He made certain she never had to walk to her car in the dark, that she never lifted anything too heavy, and Debbie had told her how Jason nearly got into a fight with a delivery man when the guy, seeing Val in shorts and a halter top, made a crude remark.

And every so often she caught Jason looking at her, a hungry longing in his eyes. Knowing that he wanted her, yet acted so indifferent, irritated her. How could a man be so blind? And why couldn't she fix his vision?

Most of the volunteers worked only on the weekends, but Val tried to stop by every day after work. She was surprised one evening when she found Jason sitting on the porch steps, staring out into space. "Rough day?" she asked, sitting beside him.

He grunted.

"Want to talk about it?"

She got a sidelong glance. "What's there to talk about?"

An evening breeze carried the aroma of the wild sweet peas climbing up the porch railing, and a fly buzzed around her head. She said nothing, content to sit beside him.

Again he glanced her way. The quick flick of his gaze caught her looking at him, and his scowl made her smile.

Jason, she'd learned, was a stickler for detail, and when things didn't go the way he wanted, he got very quiet rather than violent. The best thing to do, she'd discovered, was wait. Sooner or later he would talk.

It didn't take long that evening. "See this?" he said, holding up his right hand and wiggling his fingers. "When God designed the hand, he kept it simple. Pull one way, and the finger bends. Pull the opposite direction, and it straightens." His index finger curled over, then straightened. "A simple hydraulic pump creates the same motion. I've been putting hydraulic pumps together since I was a kid. I got a ten-foot dinosaur to move its hands. So why can't I get those hands upstairs to look like something more than sticks?"

"You probably didn't have to use hydraulic pumps put together from used parts, and I'm sure the framework for your dinosaur's fingers wasn't hair curlers covered with vinyl. Jason, those hands look good. If we keep the lights low, people aren't going to notice the motion is jerky. Besides, we don't need real, we need scary, and that jerky motion is scary."

Jason looked at her. The fading sunlight filtering through the treetops caught the golden highlights in her hair and gave a sparkle to her eyes. She was so different from Karen, yet in many ways, so like her. Slowly he smiled.

"You don't believe me, do you?" she said defensively.

"On the contrary, you're right. I'm worrying about things I shouldn't be worrying about. Karen was always getting after me for that."

Val looked out toward the ticket booth under construction. "Do you think of her often?"

"Not often, but sometimes." He also thought about Val. Far more often than he should. "You're like her in many ways."

She turned to stare at him, and he knew he'd surprised her. "How?" she asked.

With a quick, appraising glance, he tried to pinpoint the physical similarities. Actually there were few. Karen had been tall and willowy, and though her blond hair hadn't been natural, he'd only known her as a blonde. "She had blue eyes."

They just weren't as vibrant a blue as Val's. "And she had the same—" He was going to say, the same size breasts, but he stopped himself. He remembered too clearly the feel of Val's breasts, how they cushioned to his touch, and the memory brought a tightening in his loins. He looked away. "She worried about other people, like you do."

"I don't worry about other people," Val said.

"Sure you do. You make sure no one's feelings are

being hurt, you bring iced tea and lemonade for the workers, and more than once I've seen you take time to talk to someone who looked down in the dumps. The difference is, you have more self-confidence than Karen ever did."

"Me?"

He nodded. "Karen had a lot of insecurities. That's what made her inability to have children a major problem. She felt she'd let me down."

"And how did you feel?"

"I never cared. I married her because I loved her, not because I wanted children. I told her that, but . . ." He looked away again, remembering how many times he had insisted it didn't matter and wondering if he could have said it better, if staying with her might have made a difference.

Val touched his arm. "When it comes to insecurities, I've got my share. I think everyone has insecurities."

Jason tried not to let the soft feel of her fingers bother him, tried to ignore the warmth of her skin, just as he'd been ignoring the sweet scent of her ever since she'd sat down. It was just lust, he told himself as his body stirred with arousal. A physical need that hadn't been satisfied since the night he'd been with her.

An awareness showed in her eyes, the blue darkening to the hue of the evening sky. Without meaning to, he glanced at her mouth, remembering the feel of her lips. Three months hadn't lessened the desire. Just as he had the first time he saw her, he wanted her. Only now the desire was stronger. Now he knew her as a person, and he liked who she was.

Quickly he stood. "Time to get back to work. Think

you could get that second downstairs room completely cleared out while I work upstairs?"

She looked up at him. "If that's what you want."

What he wanted was to take her to bed, to make love to her through the night . . . for a thousand nights to come. Telling her he didn't care hadn't lessened the feelings. He was beginning to wonder if anything ever would.

August swept over the mountains like a hot breath. The danger of fire was high and the volunteers' kids spent most of their time at the haunted house complaining about the heat. Everyone needed a break, and Val proclaimed Slaterville's upcoming annual celebration a day off from working on the house. In fact, she told everyone to take the entire weekend off. Not that she wouldn't still be working.

Her job, however, would be at the dunk tank that WIN was sponsoring. During the previous month she had solicited volunteers and made up the schedule. Getting Jason to say yes hadn't been easy, yet he'd had to agree that his being there would bring in extra money— money they needed to buy materials to finish the house.

Sunday night, a week before the celebration day, she was afraid he was backing out. "I'm going to L.A. for a few days," he announced as they were cleaning up.

He'd gone once before and had been away for ten days. "What about Saturday?" she asked.

"I'll be back by then," he said. "I just need to connect with Bud and see a friend at FX Unlimited."

She knew he'd tried, unsuccessfully, to see Bud on his previous trip and that FX Unlimited was the special effects company he'd worked for. There was little she could say but "Good luck."

"What time am I scheduled for that dunk tank?"

"Two o'clock."

He nodded. "I'll be back Friday night."

All day Friday Val felt uneasy. That morning, before she left for work, she received a call from her mother. The news her mother shared wasn't good. Mike would soon be out of jail.

Yet Val sensed it was more than her ex-husband's release that had her edgy. All through the day, thoughts of Jason kept crossing her mind. She told herself she was being silly, that nothing was wrong, but she couldn't shake the feeling that something was. At seven o'clock that night she called his house, then again every hour after that until she gave up at midnight. Each unanswered ring intensified her fears.

She didn't sleep well.

Her alarm went off at seven, and she arose sleepy-eyed and groggy. The day had dawned sunny and warm, only a few wispy clouds drifting over the mountain peaks. It was a perfect day for Slaterville's annual celebration. She just hoped it was perfect in other ways.

Twice she had her hand on the phone to call Jason, and twice she stopped herself. What would she say if he answered? That she'd been worried? That she wasn't in love with him, but she'd spent most of the night praying he was all right?

And what if he didn't answer?

The last time he'd come back from L.A., he'd been like a kid who'd just visited a toy factory. Getting him to talk hadn't been difficult that week. He'd described the new computer-generated animations and graphics he'd seen, the innovative materials being used for models, and the advancements in stop-motion animation. He'd also mentioned a job offer.

He had told her he was a man who loved challenges. What if getting back into the business presented more of a challenge than finishing a haunted house?

She slipped on a two-piece swimsuit, then covered it with shorts and a T-shirt. If Jason didn't come back, what would she do? Like it or not, she was in love with him. In love with a man afraid to love her.

He just had to come back.

She knew parking spaces would be scarce in town, so she walked down the hillside, waving to neighbors as she passed their houses. A squirrel scampered across the road ahead of her, and bumblebees buzzed around scented flowers.

Though many of the businesses, including hers, would be closed that day, Slaterville was already teeming with activity by the time she reached the center of town. What they were celebrating on this first Sunday in August, no one really knew, but then, Slaterville wasn't known as a town that made sense. Most towns weren't named after a crook, but Slaterville had been.

William Slater had been a fast-talking store clerk who'd earned the trust of the miners in Camp Downieville. The year was 1850, and the problem was getting gold to a place where it could be sold. Back then there were no roads or express service. Slater had said he knew someone in San Francisco who would pay twenty-two dollars an ounce. The last anyone saw of him and the twenty-five thousand dollars in gold dust and nuggets the miners had given him to sell "below," was at the Isthmus of Panama.

The forefathers of Slaterville decided to name their camp after William Slater to remind foolish miners to hold on to what was theirs. Somehow even that lesson had been lost over the years. Slaterville's annual celebration certainly didn't promote the holding on to of money, but rather the spending of it. All along the town's main street and throughout the town's park, there were food booths, tables with items for sale, games of chance, and games of fun. WIN's dunk tank was one of the most popular spots. People enjoyed the opportunity to dunk others, and along with Jason, Val had managed to sign up the high school principal, the football coach, and the mayor. Nevertheless, she knew Jason's presence that year would be the big draw.

By noon the temperature was in the mid-eighties, the sun was beating down on the town, and Val was glad she'd be in the dunk tank in an hour. It wasn't going to bother her in the least bit to get wet. What did bother her was the fact that she still hadn't seen Jason. No one had.

At five to one, Debbie came on duty, relieving Maybell Jackson, who had been taking the money and giving out tickets. Right away Debbie checked the schedule to see who was on deck. "You, then Jason?" she asked Val.

While a teenage boy threw the last of his softballs at the target in an attempt to dunk Calvin Warner, the high school principal, Val pulled off her T-shirt and shorts and slipped out of her sandals. "I hope that's the lineup," she answered. "Jason didn't come back last night, and I haven't seen him today."

Debbie's eyebrows rose. "How do you know he didn't come back last night?"

Val knew she'd put her foot in her mouth, so there was no sense denying what she'd said. "I called his place . . . to remind him of what time he was on here."

A thunk, then a whoop of joy and a splash signaled the boy had succeeded in hitting the target and sending the principal into the tank. Val glanced around the crowd of people wandering the sidewalks and the park. "I didn't try him this morning. Maybe he's back and there are just so many people around, he's staying in hiding until the last minute."

"He'll show up," Debbie assured her. Val hoped she was right.

From one to two, sitting on her perch above the tank of water, Val taunted the people walking by, goading them into paying a dollar for three tries to dunk her. Each time someone missed, she taunted more. Each time a hit was made, she came out of the water laughing and sputtering.

But inside she wasn't laughing.

The closer it got to two o'clock, the more concerned she became about Jason. "I don't think he's coming," she finally said to Debbie.

"He's got two more minutes."

Val shook her head. "Something's happened." She'd known it the day before, she just hadn't wanted to believe it.

"So what are you going to do?"

"I don't know. Keep sitting here, I guess."

"I'll sit up there," Debbie's stepson, Billy, offered.

"I think not," Debbie said, squelching the idea. "I need you to hand out the balls."

"Ah, geez," the boy pouted, looking back at Val for help.

"You think I'm giving up a chance to stay cool for you, Billy?" she said, laughing. "No way."

But she would have gladly given up her place for Jason. She would have given anything to look down the street and see him. It was more than his missing his assigned time and disappointing the people who'd come with hopes of dunking him. Something was wrong, and she didn't know what to do about it.

At a quarter of three Val saw Jim Verhart, the district's high school football coach and self-proclaimed most eligible bachelor, heading her way. Watching him strut toward the dunk tank, she couldn't help but compare him to Jason. Jim had asked her out several times, but she'd never been attracted to him. There wasn't the chemistry she felt with Jason, none of the fascination.

If Jim hadn't shown up for his scheduled time, she wouldn't have cared.

"Don't get in over your head!" he yelled at her as he neared the tank.

Just then a softball connected with the target, and Val felt the seat fall out from beneath her. Once again she went into the water, holding her breath as she went under. As she climbed out, her dripping curls hanging down the sides of her face, she could hear Jim's brassy laugh.

"What happened to Mr. Hollywood?" he asked, glancing around. "I thought he was on before me. I was hoping to show him a few of my fastball special effects."

"He was a no-show," Debbie answered.

"Probably went back to Hollywood," Jim said.

The knot in Val's stomach tightened, and she was

glad when Jim took her place. As soon as she'd pulled on her shorts, T-shirt, and sandals, she jogged up the hill to her house, then drove to Jason's.

There wasn't a sign of life—no Jeep parked outside his garage, no blinds open or drapes drawn. The house looked as it had when she'd first met him, dark and foreboding, only this time no one responded to her knock on the door. She drove away with no answers and an empty sensation in the pit of her stomach.

By evening she was ready to call every hospital and police department between Slaterville and L.A. She certainly didn't want to go to the dance being held that night, only she had no choice. She'd agreed to help at the concession stand. It was a payback for thirty candle-like lightbulbs.

A few strokes with a hair pick repaired the damage of two hours of multiple dunkings, and makeup covered the strain of worry. She slipped into the most colorful sundress she owned, needing its brightness, strapped on a pair of sandals, and headed for the town hall.

The council members had done the decorating, and helium-filled balloons, crepe-paper streamers, and hanging flower baskets lent a festive atmosphere to the otherwise drab rectangular room. A food table was set up in one corner with tanks of soda behind it. A six-ounce cup sold for fifty cents. The cookies, for as long as they lasted, were free. Considering the way some of the younger boys were snitching them off the plates, Val knew they wouldn't last long.

She relieved Edith Jones, who had worked the first shift. Taking her place behind the table, Val glanced around the room. In one corner a quartet was playing. The fiddler and guitarists were almost half a century apart in age, and from their intense expressions, they were dueling over which was the better musician. Along the walls people of all ages stood talking. Only a few couples danced in the middle of the room.

It looked as though most of the town of Slaterville was in attendance, along with a handful of tourists and residents of neighboring towns. Val forced a smile and did her job. She took money and gave out drinks, but her mind was not on her task, or on the dance. All she wanted was for her shift to end so she could leave. She wasn't sure why, but she felt she needed to be by her phone, that Jason would call . . . that someone would call.

Every minute became an eternity. More than anything, she wanted to see Jason walk through the doors. He could go back to Hollywood if he wanted; she just wanted to know he was all right.

"How 'bout a dance?" a male voice asked.

Blankly she stared at Jim Verhart.

"I won't take no for an answer." He held out his hand.

He was smiling confidently, and she was glad for an excuse. "I can't. I'm working."

"Jenni will stand in for you." He nodded toward a high school girl standing by the table. "Won't you, Jenni?"

"Ah . . . yeah, sure, Mr. Verhart," Jenni answered, blushing.

"I can't," Val said again, but found herself being pulled out onto the dance floor.

"Jim, don't you know what the word 'can't' means?" she asked, stumbling.

"Coaches don't believe in that word . . . or

'never.'" He turned and took her into his arms. "Come on now, honey, you know you've been watching me all night."

"I have not." The idea was ridiculous, and she refused to follow his lead. Instead, she stood where she was.

"You have too," he returned, making a turn and forcing her to take a step just to keep her balance. "At least for most of the last hour."

"For the last hour I've been serving drinks."

"And watching me." He grinned. "Every time I looked your way, you were staring at me."

"I've been watching the doors." He continued dancing, and she reluctantly followed. "I've been looking for Jason."

"Now, what does that guy have that I don't have?"

"Humility, for one thing."

"I'm humble. You just haven't noticed."

She laughed at the idea.

"You don't know what you're missing by not going out with me."

She had a pretty good idea. "What? The plague?"

He laughed, and she joined him, then he glanced over her head, toward the doors. "He's here."

Val was afraid to hope. "Who?"

"Mr. Special Effects."

She stopped dancing and turned toward the doorway. Immediately she saw him. Standing a head taller than most of the others in the room, he was frowning, his dark gaze riveted on her.

Jason's white shirt was rumpled, the sleeves rolled up to his elbows and the first two buttons open. His slacks looked as though he'd slept in them, and a day's growth of beard covered his chin. He wasn't wearing his hat, and just above his left temple was a bandage. What concerned her the most was how the area around his left eye looked almost purple.

She pulled away from Jim and worked her way between dancing couples to where Jason stood. Stopping in front of him, she pointed toward the bandage. "What happened?"

"A wall ran into me. I'm sorry about this afternoon, about not making it."

He sounded tired, and she wanted to talk to him alone, away from all the ears tuned their way. "Don't go away," she ordered. "I've got to do something, then I'll be right back."

At the refreshment table, Val talked Jenni into working the remainder of her shift. As soon as she was back by Jason's side, she slipped her arm through his. "Let's get out of here."

To her surprise, he didn't pull away or argue.

A few people stood outside, escaping the heat and noise in the crowded hall. Each smiled and said something in greeting. Val knew there would be gossip, that by tomorrow morning her name would once again be linked with Jason's. It might upset him, but she didn't care. Keeping her hold on his arm, she guided him toward the town park. There they would have some privacy.

A breeze whipped her gathered skirt around her legs and mussed her curls. She said nothing until they were well out of hearing distance. Beneath the massive branches of an oak, she stopped and faced him. "For the last two days I've had a feeling something was wrong. Now you show up looking like you went twelve rounds with a heavyweight and tell me you ran into a wall. What really happened?"

Jason glanced down at her upturned face. She did seem concerned, yet only a few minutes ago he'd seen her laughing and dancing with another man. The jealousy that had slashed through him was scary. For more than three months he'd tried to deny he felt anything for Val. In all honesty he would have told people they were friends, that's all. Yet he recognized the green-eyed monster. He'd felt this way twice before—and both times something had happened. Something deadly.

"I called you," he said defensively. "About an hour ago."

"I had to be here."

"To dance with the football coach?"

"I was working, and he asked me to dance. It wasn't my idea."

And it was none of his business, but Jason couldn't let it go. "The way you were laughing, you didn't seem opposed to the idea."

"We were discussing humility." She let go of his arm and stepped back. "Why should it matter anyway, Jason? You and I have no future. You were the one who said that. Remember?"

He remembered, and she was right. He'd set the rules.

"It doesn't matter," he lied. "Nothing matters. I just wanted to apologize for not making it today."

He started to turn away, but she grabbed his hand, stopping him. "What happened to your head?"

He stared at the slender fingers grasping his. The pounding in his temple was nowhere near as painful as the ache in his heart. Her touch was a caress, her nearness a temptation. He wanted to bury himself in her and forget the past.

Frustrated, he pulled his hand free. "Like I said, a wall hit me."

"How? When? Where?"

Too tired to evade her questions, he decided it was easier to answer. "Yesterday morning. About an hour before I was going to drive back. I was with Kevin Bressner, and a part of a set he'd been working on fell over."

"A wall." She understood. "You have stitches?"

"Ten."

"A concussion?"

"A slight one, I guess."

"And quite a shiner."

Stepping close, she reached up and gently touched the side of his face near his eye. He stood without moving, the need to feel her touch, to inhale the sweet fragrance of her, overriding his better judgment. His arms ached to hold her, but he kept them by his sides. He shouldn't have come. He knew that. He simply couldn't stop himself.

"What about your friend?" she asked.

"A broken arm. We were both lucky. I remember a similar accident happening three years ago, when I was in England. That time, a grip was killed."

In her eyes he saw concern. "*You* could have been killed," she said. "All day yesterday I was afraid something had happened."

He'd thought of her often in the last thirty-six hours. Thought about her faith in his innocence, her trust and how he'd hurt her. He'd thought he could push her to the back of his mind, ignore his feelings.

He'd failed.

Somehow he'd grown even more attracted to her in the last three months, mere physical appeal turning to deeper feelings. He'd expected her to mope after the brutal way he'd called an end to their affair. Instead, she'd acted as though nothing had happened, as if they'd never been more than good friends. She'd kept him off guard, and every day he'd found himself looking forward to seeing her, talking with her.

"I was told not to drive last night," he said. "So I hit the road early this morning. I would have made it up here by two if I hadn't gotten a flat less than a hundred miles out of L.A. And, of course, I didn't have a spare. By the time I got a new tire on, I knew I'd be pushing it to make it by two, but I still thought I could do it. Next thing I knew, blue lights were flashing behind me."

"Oh, no," she groaned.

"I spent most of the afternoon in a two-bit sergeant's office."

"For a speeding ticket?"

"For being Jason McLain, the man who got away with murder."

"They can't do that."

He laughed at her idealism. "They did it." He touched her face, needing the contact. "Look, I'm sorry I bothered you tonight. You go on back inside. Have a good time. I just wanted you to know why I wasn't there this afternoon."

He started to pull his hand back, but she caught it, a feather-light grip of steel holding his fingers to her cheek. "Where are you going?" she asked.

"Home."

"Let me go with you."

He understood what she was offering and wanted to say yes. Buried in her body, he could find the solace he needed, the strength to go on. She alone could chase the demons away.

But for how long?

Never before had the word "no" been so difficult to say.

NINE

Sunday morning Val woke to weather so opposite to the day before, she couldn't believe it. The wind had brought in a storm front. Staring at the rain coming down, she shook her head.

At nine o'clock she tried calling Jason. To make sure he was all right, she told herself. After eight rings she decided he wasn't answering his phone or wasn't home. She dressed for church and got into her car. On a whim she drove the opposite direction, past Jason's house. As far as she could tell, he wasn't there.

The church she'd been attending ever since she'd moved to Slaterville was in the middle of town; nevertheless, she drove past the Clifford house. She knew she would be late when she saw Jason's Jeep parked in the gravel lot. She also knew she had to see him.

The rain was coming down in a torrent when she got out of her car. Grabbing her umbrella, she made a run for the house.

The moment she stepped inside, she knew how tourists would feel when they entered. The windows were now all boarded up, and the only lighting came from the incandescent bulbs that ran along the baseboard, illuminating the path to be followed. Closing her umbrella, she leaned it against the wall, then shut the outside door, cutting off all natural light.

"Jason!" she called.

"Who's there?"

His answer came from the back of the house, and she started in that direction, passing the game room, where an assortment of card-playing miners and their ladies idly waited for the final wires and levers that were needed to activate their moving parts. The house was cool, its emptiness eerie. "Jason?" she called again, then saw him.

He was standing in the middle of the second room, wearing a T-shirt, jeans, and running shoes. What she noticed most was the gun belt around his waist and the gun strapped to his leg.

"You're a dirty cheat," he said, walking toward her. "That's what you are."

She gasped when he drew his gun and pointed it at her.

The bang echoed through the house and her head, and she stumbled back, stunned.

She'd been shot.

Jason had shot her. He'd called her a cheat and had shot her.

Looking down at her chest, she expected to see blood on her dress. Any moment now she would feel the pain. As close as he was, he couldn't have missed.

"So what do you think?" Jason asked, stepping out of the next room down the hall. "Seem convincing?"

He looked different from a minute before. He was

now wearing a gray sweatshirt and khaki shorts, a growth of beard covered his cheeks and jaw, and the bandage was still on his forehead, his eye still purplish. There wasn't a gun to be seen.

"Jason?" Stepping forward, she looked into the first room.

Again she triggered the sensor under the carpet in the hallway, restarting the sequence. A clean-shaven, unmarred Jason—wearing a white T-shirt and jeans—faced her. His lips moved and he drew his gun. She saw the smoke come from the barrel. The only things missing this time were his spoken words and the bang.

"I haven't got the dialogue and sound effects on the tape so it loops," Jason explained. "And I won't be the one doing this. We just wanted to see if I could get the laser projectors set up so they worked. Today I'll call Kevin and tell him all's okay, and he'll get an actor to dress up like a miner and go through the sequence."

"It's a hologram," Val muttered to herself, finally understanding.

"Fool you?"

"Fool me?" She marched toward Jason, glaring. "Fool me? It scared me to death. You're just lucky I didn't die of fright. How would you have explained that?" Both angry and relieved, she shook a fist at him.

He laughed, stopping her by placing his hands on her shoulders. "I guess it did fool you."

"I thought I was dead."

Suddenly he stopped laughing, and the silence in the house grew heavy. Only the wind whistling through cracks in the siding and the rain beating against the boarded windows broke the stillness. She knew what she'd said and what he was thinking. If she could, she would have taken back her words.

"It's just that it seemed so real," she said, trying to explain.

He pulled his hands away from her shoulders. "And I was jealous last night."

"I know you wouldn't really—" She stopped, realizing what he'd confessed. Smiling, she cocked her head. "You were?"

His back straightened, and she knew he hadn't meant to reveal his feelings. He turned away without answering her question and walked into the room with the hologram. She followed.

"Look at me," she ordered.

He ignored her, going over to one of the laser projectors. Standing to the side, he checked its angle.

She wasn't about to be ignored. "For three months —over three months—you've been putting me through hell. Maybe you can pretend you don't feel anything, but I love you."

He continued playing with the projector. "Well, you shouldn't."

"Why not?" She walked up beside him. "Because you're going to kill me?"

Straightening, he faced her. "How do you know I won't?"

"Because you wouldn't."

"This isn't a fantasy," he said bitterly. "How do I make you understand that, Val? Friday Kevin was hurt. It hasn't stopped. Accidents happen around me. People die."

"But you're not the cause."

"That's not what the sergeant who detained me yesterday said."

"He doesn't know you."

"And you do?" He scoffed. "What kind of a judge of human nature are you? You married a man who abused you. Went back to him. You're living in this ghost town because you're afraid you'll go back to him again."

"That's not why I'm living here."

"I can hurt you, Val. Really hurt you. Do you know why the police were so sure I'd killed my wife? Because everything pointed to me. I had access to the safe and access to Karen's gun. I've set up dozens of gags using triggering devices with guns. With no fingerprints in the house other than Karen's, the maid's, and mine, and no way anyone could have gotten into the safe, other than Karen or me opening it, who else could have done it? I wasn't just the prime suspect, I was the only suspect. The only thing I don't understand is why that jury acquitted me."

"Because they didn't think you had a motive."

His eyes narrowed slightly. "But you know different, don't you?"

"I know there's a chance someone else got into that safe and rigged that gun. If your wife had an affair, there was another man."

Jason shook his head. "But she didn't meet with him at the house. I asked my lawyer to check on that, to see if Karen had been seeing anyone while I was gone. He thought it a reasonable request, but found that other than a few friends who'd stopped by for visits, the only people who'd been in our house from the time I was in England to Karen's death were Karen, the maid, and me."

"Friends?" she repeated suspiciously.

"These were people we've known for years, and not one of them was someone Karen would have had an affair with. I know that for a fact."

"So she was meeting this man away from your house?"

"Evidently. She must have been very discreet."

"Or lied about having an affair."

"And why would she do that?"

"If she wanted out of the marriage. Do you think your wife might have been rigging the gun for you? Could it have fired accidentally?"

From his stunned expression, she guessed he'd never considered that possibility. "And why would she want to kill me?"

"To get out of the marriage."

He shook his head. "Karen didn't want out. If she had, why tell me the affair had been a mistake and was over?"

"Jason, she could have been lying to you."

"No," he said firmly. "I could always tell when Karen was lying. Give it up, Val. The finger keeps pointing back at me."

He walked out of the room, but she stood where she was. All of her strategies for making him fall in love with her were worthless if he continued to believe he was a killer. There had to be something that would clear his mind of the guilt.

She found him in the next room, tearing open a box. "We need to find your wife's killer."

He paused as she came up beside him. "We?"

"You and me. Look, I know what it's like to be a

victim. Helplessness is not a fun state. You need to take some kind of action."

He shook his head again and went back to opening the box. "What we have to do is get this place finished."

The projectors for the hologram hadn't been in place the last time she'd been in the house, and lying beside the box he was opening lay the mannequin they'd begged from a dress shop in Grass Valley. In its right arm socket a universal joint was now in place. It hadn't been there before. "How long have you been over here?" she asked.

With a shrug of his broad shoulders, Jason pulled a lever from the box. "I couldn't sleep last night."

"So you came here?"

"It was better than thinking." He pulled out another lever and a long strand of wire. "These are the cable controls I needed from Bud. I got hold of him the second day I was there." Jason smiled when he glanced her way. "He asked about you."

"I'm surprised he even remembered me."

"Oh, he remembered. You have a way with men."

She wished. She didn't seem to be doing very well at the moment. "Did you find out why you could never get in touch with him?"

"I guess he's run into problems with *Raptors II*. The director didn't like the morfing—" He paused to explain. "That's where one thing or person changes into something else, like the evil Terminator in *Terminator 2*. Or like in those television ads you see where one face becomes another and then another.

"Anyway, morfing is all computer generated, and can really be effective if it comes out right. What Bud's been working on isn't working, and neither are his models. Evidently, on film, they're creating bogus effects. He had to go over to England last month and make a lot of changes, and even now he's afraid he might not be able to deliver on time. The guy's under a lot of stress, and wasn't too happy to see me. Though he said it was great that I was working on something and that he knew all along I wouldn't be able to stay away from special effects, I think he's worried that I might step in on his territory."

"And would you?" Was *Raptors II* the film that would take him from Slaterville, the haunted house, and her?

He shook his head. "I assured him I was plenty busy with this house and had a delivery date of my own to meet. But I can understand the problems he's having. I ran into one after another with the original movie."

Pulling out more wires and levers, he lay them on the floor. "Once these are connected to the wires running downstairs, our gambling miners and their women will be ready to go into action."

"Bit by bit it's all coming together, isn't it?"

"I should have my part done by the end of August." He gave her a sidelong glance. "Then the rest will be up to you and your committee. I don't think you'll have any problems."

She didn't like the way he was talking. "You make it sound as though you won't be around."

For a moment he looked deep into her eyes, then his dark gaze switched back to the box. "I'm thinking of moving."

The fear that had been building within her took shape, turning solid and twisting in her stomach. "Back to L.A.?"

"No, not L.A."

"Then where? Why?"

He kept his eyes focused on the box, and his words came slowly. "I'm not sure where. I just feel it would be better if I moved."

"Better?" She knew it wouldn't be better for her. "Now who's running and hiding?"

His head snapped up. "Val, I was jealous last night."

"Well, you shouldn't have been."

"But I was. I've tried to keep you safe, but—"

"What are you going to do, put a cocoon around me? I stubbed my toe last week. Is that your fault? Mike is getting out of jail next week. Is that your fault?"

Concern immediately filled his eyes, and Jason touched her arm. "Do you think he'll come see you?"

After what her mother had told her Friday morning, it was a real possibility. "He knows where I live. I don't know how, but someone must have told him. He might show up."

"And if he does?"

Val wasn't sure what would happen, but she knew one thing for certain. "You were wrong earlier. I'm not worried about going back to him. And I'm not hiding out in this town. Maybe once I was a victim and running scared, but I've changed." And she knew why. "After knowing you, how could I find Mike attractive?"

She said it with conviction, but Jason wasn't entirely convinced. Once she saw the man, she might change her mind. And how would he react if she did? Here he'd gotten jealous simply seeing her in the arms of a high school coach he knew she didn't like.

She brushed his forehead with her fingertips, tracing

the edge of his bandage. Her caress was as tender as a lover's kiss. Soothing. Exciting.

"Does your head hurt?" she asked.

"Just a little."

"Were you really jealous?"

He wanted to deny it, but couldn't. "Yes . . . but I don't think there's any problem."

Her laughter had the gentleness of a lark's song. "Jason, there's never been any problem. Jim Verhart is one man you don't have to be jealous of." She trailed her fingertips down the side of his face, tracing the stubble of two days of no shaving. "The only man I'm interested in is you."

Sensations of need shot through him, and he pulled back, away from her touch. "You shouldn't be."

"Because you're dangerous to be around?" Her smile showed her lack of fear. "I've known that from the very beginning."

"You're not taking this seriously." He took a step back, upset with the way his body kept reacting to her nearness.

"Oh, I'm very serious," she said, continuing to pursue him. "What upsets me is how we've wasted the last three months."

His back hit the wall, stopping his retreat. Grinning like a cat that had cornered its prey, she moved in, her hips touching his. Immediately what had been soft grew hard, and he knew she could tell. Words of denial weren't going to do him a damned bit of good.

"It's just lust," he lied.

"So?" Her hands slipped under his sweatshirt and he sucked in a breath, tightening his abdominal muscles.

"You deserve more," he said, knowing he wasn't going to be able to resist touching her much longer. Keeping his hands by his sides was becoming an impossibility.

"Lust is fine." She lifted his sweatshirt, baring his chest. Dipping her head, she kissed him, her mouth butterfly soft.

Her lips were cool, his skin hot. He'd shot effects where opposites collided. One always fell apart. Jason fell apart.

Placing his hands on her shoulders, he drew her back and scanned her face. Diamonds of light shimmered in her eyes, giving them a sparkle, while excitement painted a blush on her cheeks. He focused on her lips, on the satisfied smile that curved them upward.

She'd won and she knew it.

Slowly he lowered his head, feeling her rise on her toes.

Bud had been surprised when Jason had said there was nothing going on between him and Val. "I was sure something would develop," he'd said. "Man, that day you two met, the electricity was snapping all over the place."

The electricity was there now.

The passion.

He'd created a wall, but she'd broken through it. Holding her, tasting her, he knew he could never step back. As if in a stop-motion sequence, he claimed every part of her mouth. Like layers of film that created a whole, he discovered the layers of a kiss—its gentleness and intensity, its sweetness and passion.

He nibbled a fine line down the side of her neck, then licked his way back. In his arms she shivered, and he heard her soft moan.

"I've missed this," he confessed in a husky whisper. "Missed the softness of you."

With one hand he sought out the softest part of her, letting his fingers travel over the front of her dress. Buttons fell open, the two sides parting to expose velvety skin and a silken bra. Through the sleek material, he felt the curve of one breast, then the other, each nipple pebbling at his touch.

Shaking fingers opened the clasp, and he pushed everything aside, baring her to her waist. As he stared at her, an uncontrolled heat raced through his loins, and it was his turn to groan.

She was sweetness and softness, yet there was a resilience to her. He didn't deserve her, but he needed her. With her there was no hype, no phoniness. She was a slash of light in a world of darkness.

Val watched Jason's eyes. Day after day she looked into eyes, checking optic nerves and blood vessels. How much more there was to see when you looked with your heart. He could call what he felt for her whatever he liked, but what she saw was love.

He bent his head, playing kisses down her shoulder to the rise of a breast. She wanted to mew when he licked her, to whimper when he sucked in a nipple. Electricity coursed through her, igniting responses throughout her body. The moment would be burned in her memory.

This was what she'd yearned for every day of the last three months, what she'd dreamed of each night. The firm touch of his mouth, the sinewy strength of his arms, and the gentle, seducing caresses of his hands.

Frustration and anger were replaced by desire. She swept her hands over his back, holding him close and massaging his shoulders. His sweatshirt was a barrier, keeping her from him, and she slipped her fingers under the cotton, loving the heat of his skin, the spring of his ribs, and the curve of his spine. In his arms she felt small and vulnerable and yet so safe.

His mouth sought hers again, the invasion of his tongue sending out a shock of anticipation. The need growing deep inside of her was one she knew he could satisfy. Wantonly she again rubbed her hips against his, answering his unspoken question.

Inch by inch he drew her skirt up her legs to her hips. She felt the cotton of his shorts against her bare thighs as his fingers slipped inside her panties. "We should have put a bed in this place," he said huskily, his breathing none too steady.

"You said a man with a good imagination could create special effects out of practically nothing."

"Throwing my words back at me, are you?" He glanced around the room. "Well, you've heard of four on the floor. How about two? There is that carpeting remnant."

She looked at the piece of leftover carpeting lying in the corner and nodded. "Won't be the first time we've done it on the carpet. But what if someone comes?"

"Comes?" He chuckled suggestively, then let her skirt fall back around her knees. "I'll lock the front door, then we'll take care of that."

With the house's windows boarded up, she wasn't worried about anyone seeing in, but the door to the hallway had been removed. There was no way to ensure privacy if someone did enter the house. It would be risky, but, the risk itself had an appeal that sent Val's heart racing.

She was sitting on the generous rectangle of carpet when Jason came back into the room. She'd taken off her sandals, but that was all. Watching him near, she felt a fluttering in her stomach. Was this an illusion or reality?

He sat beside her and began unlacing his shoes. "All locked up. Not that anyone should show up. We did say we were taking this weekend off."

"True, but then again, you and I are here."

"That we are."

His sweatshirt went after his shoes and socks, the springy dark hairs covering his chest begging for her touch. He smiled when she pressed her palm against him, then he turned and helped her remove her dress.

Her slip and panties went as quickly, then his shorts and briefs. He paused only long enough to get a packet from his wallet. Not until they were both naked did he kiss her. Stretching his body out beside hers, he began his assault.

He kissed and he licked, nipped then suckled, until she was writhing with need and kissing him was no longer enough. Feeling him rubbing against her wasn't enough. She wanted him inside her, filling her and satisfying her. She wanted his heart and his soul, to know he was a part of her and that he would never leave.

His body was slick with perspiration when he sat back and looked down at her. His eyes half-veiled, his breathing heavy, he touched her between her legs, and she nearly exploded.

"Jason, please," she begged, her body at his mercy.

"You give so much," he said hoarsely, and took what she offered.

Their bodies entwined, they moved as one, each

thrust of his accepted and matched by her. Breathing became an impossibility, time was suspended. Reality turned into an illusion, past and future forgotten.

A wild cry escaped from her throat, and she knew its cause. The right spot had been reached, perfection found. Pleasure rocketed through her body in a series of tiny explosions.

He followed her path, finding his own satisfaction, and she watched his face, marveling that she could give him the same elation he gave her. The tears that dampened her cheeks were tears of joy, the lump in her throat from pure happiness. For a while, at least, he was hers—a part of her life. For a while she could make him forget his doubts.

Slowly he eased himself out of her and nestled beside her. His kiss was tender, his sigh one of satisfaction. "Why does something that's so wrong feel so right?"

"Because it's not wrong." She had to convince him of that.

"I wish I could believe you," he said, cradling her face in his hands.

"You can. You've got to forget the past."

He kissed her, long and tenderly, then rubbed his hands over her back and through her hair, cuddling her close. The past, Jason knew, couldn't be forgotten. While he'd been in Los Angeles, he'd called his parents. His father had talked to him, but his mother had refused, as she'd refused ever since the night his brother died. Five years and three months of silence from the woman who had given him life. He sometimes wished he had been the one in the car that night.

"You're not a murderer," Val said, somehow reading his mind.

"Any ideas on how to prove that?" he asked.

"There's got to be something about your wife's death that no one's considered . . . or discovered. If she truly had an affair, she had to have told someone. Women do those things, keep diaries, tell friends."

"When we first got married, she had a diary." He'd forgotten that. "It had a combination lock, and she kept forgetting the sequence of numbers." Karen could never remember numbers. "I think she stopped keeping one. At least, I didn't find one when I cleaned out her things, and the police must not have found one."

"And her friends didn't say anything?" He shook his head. "Her mother?"

"Karen's parents died when she was young, and she was raised by a very strict aunt. I can't imagine her telling Aunt Eva anything, much less that she was having an affair."

"Well, someday something's going to turn up," Val promised, and traced a path through the hairs on his chest with the tip of a finger.

As her fingertip moved lower, another part of his body responded, life coming back into its limp form. He chuckled and caught her hand. "Something else is going to 'turn up' soon."

"That right?" she asked innocently, grinning.

"I take it you wouldn't be opposed?"

" 'Opposed' is the root of 'opposite,' and opposites attract," she reminded him.

Again he chuckled, kissing her forehead, then nibbling on her ear.

As intent as he was on covering Val's face with kisses, he was surprised he was aware of anything else, especially the rattling of a door. At first he didn't realize what it was he heard, not with the wind outside blowing the branches against the side of the house and shaking the rafters. He might have entirely ignored the sound if it hadn't been followed by a faint call.

Val stiffened in his embrace. "Someone's here," she whispered, pulling back.

Immediately he rolled away from her and sat up. Again he heard the muted voices, two as far as he could tell. They were calling his name . . . and Val's.

"Where are my underpants?" she asked, hysteria edging her voice.

"Here." He grabbed them, along with her dress, bra, and slip. As she frantically pulled them on, he searched for his own clothes.

They could hear footsteps crunching on the gravel along the side of the house and knew whoever it was, was walking back to the shed. The front door might be locked, but all of the workers were now familiar with the underground passageway.

Val struggled with the clasp of her bra, swearing, then pulled her half-slip on inside out. She didn't bother to reverse it, her focus on her dress. Jason might have laughed when she put a button into the wrong hole, but he was too busy trying to get his own clothes on straight and to rub out any signs of their lovemaking from the carpet remnant. Quickly he grabbed the box of levers and cables and headed for the cellar. As far as their visitors would know, they'd been so involved working on the hydraulics, they hadn't heard anything.

TEN

By the time Julia Stern and Barb Wilcox made it through the passageway, Val was threading wires down openings in the floor of the game room and Jason was in the cellar. Neither woman asked why their calls hadn't been answered or the front door opened. Julia and Barb didn't say anything but "Hi," and "Can we help?" But Jason was sure the two must have guessed what was going on. Working on animated models and hydraulics didn't put whisker burns on a woman's face or lipstick on a man's shirt.

The next night, as volunteers arrived to work on the haunted house, Jason wasn't sure how to act with Val. After what had happened the morning before, he couldn't very well pretend nothing had changed. He'd worried about it most of the day and found himself growing tenser and tenser as the evening progressed. How many of the problems he was having getting the model of Eldon Clifford to move correctly were mechanical and how many were due to his tension, he wasn't sure, but at exactly the same time he heard Val enter the house, her lilting voice and bubbly laughter carrying to him, a wire broke.

He swore, and Chad Kerns, who was working with him, looked over. "Problems?"

"Definitely," Jason answered. Problems with his life. Problems with his emotions. He had to get things under control.

His control faded the moment he saw Val. Grinning, she walked directly to his side, kissed him on the cheek, and asked if he'd missed her.

He could feel Chad's gaze on them and knew his response would be repeated to half the town of Slaterville before the night was over. Giving in, Jason smiled and hugged her, whispering so only she could hear his words. "I think you're making a mistake."

"No mistake," she whispered back.

He wasn't convinced and made certain someone else was always around while they worked together, and he left before she did that night. On Tuesday night she was the one who left first, but five minutes after he arrived home, he heard a light knock on his side door.

Even before he opened the door, he knew it was Val. "Hi," she said. "May I come in?"

"As I recall, you asked me that once before, and my saying yes is what got me into all of this work."

"And you're loving every minute of it." She cocked her head the way she often did, reminding him of a curious robin. "Well?"

"I still don't think this is a good idea," he said, but opened the door wider. "People are going to talk."

"People *are* talking," she said. "When you live in a town where nothing much happens, talk is the only thing that makes life interesting. I haven't been stoned yet."

She had it twisted. "It's me they'll be stoning."

Ignoring his grumbling, she walked through his kitchen to his living room. "We're the ones who need to talk."

"About?"

He passed her, going to the window that looked out on the road. People might be talking, but there was no sense in fueling the gossip. He'd been keeping his drapes open. He closed them.

"We need to talk about who killed your wife."

"What good is talking going to do?" He and his lawyers had talked about it endlessly. The police had talked about it. Friends. Coworkers.

Talking had convinced the police that he was guilty; his lawyers had warned him to be careful what he said; and he'd discovered what his friends said to his face wasn't the same as what they said behind his back. Talk got a person nowhere, and every time he talked to Val, they ended up on the floor.

Glancing her way, he knew he wasn't strong enough to resist the temptation. It had been two days since they'd been together, and she looked absolutely delectable in the blue shorts and white tank top she was wearing. "I think you'd better leave," he said.

"If your wife said she'd had an affair," Val said, ignoring his remark, "and you don't believe she lied, then who was the guy?"

She reminded him of a dog with a bone. She just wouldn't let it go. "I told you, I don't know. Now, will you leave?"

"Not until we talk."

Giving in, he walked over and slumped down on the sofa. "Okay, we talk. What do we say?"

"I don't know exactly." Like a kid, she curled up on the opposite end of the sofa, kicking off her sandals and bringing her feet up under her as she faced him. "But there's got to be something. Something your wife said, something you found after her murder, something . . ."

He admired her tenacity, but he had to shake his head, stopping her. "The police said the same thing when I kept insisting someone else had to have done it. Investigators went through everything in the house, through my belongings and Karen's. Hell, I've been through everything myself, at least a dozen times. And when Bud was up here in April, he basically asked me the same thing, and we looked through everything I'd kept of Karen's."

"What you kept? You didn't keep everything?" As he shook his head again, her expression turned crestfallen. "That will make things more difficult. What if you gave away the one bit of evidence that would prove you innocent?"

"Actually I don't know why I kept what I did. When the trial was over, all I wanted to do was get away and forget."

"Get away and hide," she said, and he knew she was right. That had been his motive for moving to Slaterville.

And then he'd met Val.

She moved closer, pulling her feet out from under her, and took his hand in hers. "I wish I could take your pain away."

He would ask that of no one, much less of her. Gazing at her face, he wondered what miracle had brought her to his door. She'd become his friend as well as his lover, his soul mate. The love he saw in her eyes warmed him and scared him. Once he'd accused her of not trusting him; now he hoped she wasn't too trusting.

To his surprise, she released his hand and pushed herself up from the sofa. Looking down at him, she said, "Show me the things you kept."

"You're just not going to let this drop, are you?" he grumbled, but stood and led her to a bedroom that was filled with still-unpacked boxes. "What I kept is in those."

"May I look through them?"

"Go ahead." He wasn't going to help. He'd been through those boxes when Bud was up. Once had been enough.

Leaning against a wall, he watched her dig into the first box. Doggedly she pulled out what he'd packed, her lips pursed in concentration, her gaze darting over each item as she removed it. She was interested in the contents of the box; he was interested in looking at her.

Her nipples were hard nubs pressing against her tank top; she wasn't wearing a bra. Folding his arms across his chest, he tried not to think about how soft her breasts would feel or how wonderful those nipples would taste. Nevertheless, he knew he was getting aroused, his shorts becoming uncomfortably tight, and he was almost glad when she pulled a scrapbook from one box and asked, "Was this hers?"

He nodded and pushed himself away from the wall, walking over to her. "Karen kept reviews in it, mostly from the movies she was in, a few from ones I worked on."

"I'd forgotten she was a movie star."

"Star might be an exaggeration. She had a few bit parts."

Val opened the scrapbook, flipping through the pages. Karen had kept clippings, invitations to openings and parties, and a few photos. It was strange, but looking at the pictures wasn't as painful as it once had been. Not that he didn't remember the good times or the love he'd had for Karen, it just didn't feel as strong.

"She's beautiful," Val said with a sigh.

Jason slipped an arm around her shoulders. "She was beautiful. Her problem was, she had a little-girl voice. It was great for bit parts, but never quite what casting wanted for a lead."

"I probably saw her in a movie." She pointed at a picture on the next page. "That's Bud, isn't it?"

"Good old Bud." Jason reached down and turned the page, revealing another picture of Bud, standing between Karen and him. "You'll see a lot of him throughout here. I met him about two and a half years after Karen and I were married. He was new to Hollywood, new to special effects, and scared as a pup. Both Karen and I felt sorry for him. The guy had a really rough childhood. When he was a kid, his mother ran off, abandoning him and his father. Then, when he was sixteen, his house burned down, killing his father and almost killing him."

"You worked together?"

"Sort of. He works for Magic Motion Studios, and sometimes FX Unlimited hires them to do special projects. A lot of times we'd get together at my place after work, share a few beers, and discuss gags late into the night. There were times when he practically lived at the house."

"Could he have been the man? Karen's lover?"

"No," Jason said without hesitation. "Not Bud. She felt sorry for him, but they didn't get along that well. I think it was because he was always teasing her, kidding her about her voice and about her inability to remember numbers. You know what it's like to be run down all the time."

"All too well." Val pointed to another picture of Karen with a man. "What about him?"

"That was my brother." Jason flipped the scrapbook closed. "You're grabbing at straws, Val. I've been through this, asked myself the same questions. If I were to make a guess, I'd say Karen met someone new while I was gone, maybe at the grocery store, maybe at the gas station. I'd probably been away for several weeks by then, she was feeling depressed, inadequate as a woman, and this guy made a pass. She took him up on it, they went somewhere—a motel, his place—slept together, and then she went home. That's it. It was over."

"That's what she told you?"

"No. Karen said she'd slept with another man, it was a mistake, she didn't want to talk about it, but it would never happen again." He put the scrapbook aside and pulled out a large black enamel box with a flower design. "This was one of her Chinese puzzle boxes. She collected them. Don't ask me why I kept it."

She didn't. Nor did she ask why he'd kept Karen's two other Chinese puzzle boxes. Val did ask if he knew how they worked.

Taking the smallest one, he quickly pulled it apart.

"Everything is interlocked." Just as quickly, he put it back together.

"Sort of like our lives."

He glanced at her and wondered just how interlocked their lives were. Was it chance that had brought them together . . . or fate? Setting the puzzle box down, he stared at her.

"One of your Oscars?" she asked, pulling the statue from the box. "Why don't you have this in your living room?"

"How about my bedroom?" He took the Oscar from her hands. "Come on, let's put this in my bedroom."

All the way to his room she argued that they needed to concentrate on looking through Karen's things. Somehow her arguments got weaker when he started kissing her. By the time she was standing next to his bed, his comforter and sheet still pulled back from when he had risen that morning, the only sound she was making was something akin to a purr.

"As long as you're here," Jason whispered into her ear, "I thought we'd try something different. Unless you prefer the carpet?"

The bed seemed to suit her just fine.

Val stopped by three more nights that week. Each time, she told him she was there to go through the boxes in his spare bedroom, that she was sure they would find something in one that would give them a clue. Even though he knew she'd find nothing, Jason didn't object. He actually helped her. But not once did she make it completely through a box before he got her into his bedroom. The only thing she accomplished was to move all three of his Oscars to his bedroom and all three of Karen's Chinese puzzle boxes to the living room.

On the following Wednesday Val was determined that after they finished working on the haunted house, she was going to Jason's and get through the contents of those boxes. "It's funny what a man keeps," she told Ginger. "I mean, some of the things Jason kept of his wife's make sense. I can see keeping a scrapbook and puzzle boxes if she really liked them, but he also kept a cracked flower vase and a bottle of hand lotion."

"Maybe he figured he'd get dry hands here in the mountains," Ginger said.

The street door opened, and Val automatically glanced that way. She knew no one was scheduled for a late appointment, but she half expected Jason to drop by.

She'd forgotten that there was one other person who might show up, that her ex-husband was now out of jail.

He sauntered in like a man about to stake his claim, all clean-shaven and arrogantly male in his black muscle shirt, tight-fitting black jeans, and cowboy boots. He smiled his come-hither smile, and Val remembered the way she used to melt when they were in high school and he'd meet her after work, smiling that smile. He would come to the restaurant about five minutes before the end of her shift and would smile and saunter across the room, knowing every girl in the place was watching him. And she would feel so proud because he was there for her. It didn't matter that his words had barbs and he was always running her down. She was the one he'd chosen.

That was when he was captain of the football team

and president of the senior class—before they were married and his occasional drinking binges became every-night affairs. Before his hands became battering rams.

A shudder ran through her, and she straightened. "What do you want, Mike?" she asked, keeping her tone cool.

"No 'How are you? Good to see you'?" he asked.

"The last time I saw you, you hit me."

"That was three years ago. Time to let go of the past and welcome the future." He glanced toward Ginger. "Hi, I'm the thorn in Valerie's side, once known as her husband."

"There is no future," Val said firmly, wishing she could forget the past. What had she ever seen in Mike? "At least no future between you and me. I thought we had it settled that you weren't to see me again."

He shrugged. "It's been three years. I thought you'd be interested in how I'm doing."

"I know how you're doing. You were in prison."

"I'm a different person than the guy you knew. A better person."

"Good." She meant it. She also didn't believe him.

He strolled across her waiting room, looking around. "So this is where you ended up. I'm surprised. The way you talked last time I saw you, I thought you'd be in a big fancy office raking in the dollars."

She saw no need to tell him he was the one who had ruined that dream. And maybe it wasn't Mike who'd brought her to Slaterville. Perhaps it was fate. "I like it here."

From the corner of her eye Val saw Ginger move over to the telephone and place her hand on the receiver. She shook her head slightly. Mike seemed sober; she didn't think he would cause a problem.

He stopped in front of a poster promoting eye exams. "I understand you also work in Grass Valley."

"You seem to know a lot about me." And that bothered her.

He turned away from the poster and looked at her, smiling. "You gave one of my cellmates an eye exam about a year and a half ago. Small world, isn't it?"

Too small, she decided.

When she didn't comment, Mike went on. "I talked to your mother last week."

"So she said."

"We had a nice talk. You two still always bickering?"

"Actually, since she divorced my dad, we've gotten on a lot better." Val glanced at the clock on the wall. It was five. "Was there something you wanted?"

He lifted an eyebrow suggestively and smiled again. Then he glanced at Ginger. "No, I was just passing through and thought I'd stop in and say hello, see if maybe you wanted to go out to dinner or something."

Val knew no one "passed through" Slaterville. The northern end of Highway 49 didn't lead to any towns Mike would be going to. No, he was there for one purpose—to mess up her life.

"I already have a date tonight," she said, and was glad for the excuse. She saw no need to explain that her date was another night of working with Jason on the house.

"That's too bad." Mike looked around once more, then back at her. "No time to chat about old times?"

"Sorry." She walked over to the door and opened it.

"I'm going to lock up here and be on my way. Have a nice trip, wherever you're going."

He stayed where he was, looking at the open door, then he glanced at Ginger, who remained by the phone. His smile in place, Mike walked toward Val, pausing in front of her. "Maybe we can get together some other time."

"Maybe," she lied.

"See you," he said, and surprised her with a quick kiss on the lips. He left, sauntering down the sidewalk.

For a minute Val stood where she was, too numb to think. Then she closed and locked the door. Turning to Ginger, she sighed in relief, then laughed nervously. "Boy, what a fool I was to think I ever loved him."

Ginger came around from behind the reception desk. "He is good-looking."

"Too damned good-looking." That had been her downfall in the first place.

"But it's over?"

"Yes." It felt good to say that. Liberating. It *was* over —the control Mike had had over her, the attraction that had drawn her back, time after time. Everything. "He's a part of my past, nothing more."

"You about ready to leave, then?"

"I've got to clear my desk, lock a couple of cabinets, and I'm out of here."

"Want me to stick around?" Ginger asked. "Just in case he comes back?"

Val shook her head. "I doubt he'll come back here. He'll head for my place next, only I'm not going to go home when I leave here. I'm going straight over to the Clifford house, and I just might give Sheriff Maxwell a call from there and have him check my place out."

"You going to tell Jason that Mike came by?"

"Of course."

Ginger laughed. "That ought to be interesting."

"Meaning what?"

"That I've seen the way he watches you when another man's around. I wouldn't want to be Mike."

"Jason wouldn't do anything," Val said, yet wished Ginger hadn't mentioned the possibility. Jason had been jealous of Jim Verhart. How would he feel about Mike? What would he do?

Quickly she cleared her desk and locked the cabinets. It would be better if Jason didn't know that Mike was around, but how could she not tell him? He was sure to find out. Someone would mention it.

She had to tell him, that was all there was to it.

Val was still considering the problem as she walked to her car. Just before she reached the end of the building and the parking lot, she realized someone was behind her. Instinctively she knew who it was, and for a moment considered running, then decided she was through running. Turning, she faced Mike.

"Hi again," he said, grinning.

"What are you doing here?"

His eyes crinkled in amusement. "Following you. What time's your date?"

"Right now." She glanced at her watch. "I'm late, in fact."

He kept coming toward her. "I'm sure he can wait a minute or two while you talk to your husband."

"Ex-husband," she said emphatically, forcing herself to stand where she was. "Mike, why did you come here?"

He sighed, his grin losing its cockiness and becoming almost sad. "I guess to tell you I'm sorry. I had a lot of time to think while I was in prison, time when I was sober and could think. I really messed it up with us, didn't I?"

She'd agree with him on that. Slowly she nodded.

"I want you to know I regret everything I ever did to hurt you, really I do. It wasn't me hitting you, it was some kind of monster I became."

"I know." She just never knew when the monster might appear. Even now she was watchful.

"Remember the time our senior year when I forgot I'd promised to take you to a party, and the next day I stood on my head on your lawn and begged you to forgive me?"

It seemed so long ago, but she did remember. "My dad said it showed what an idiot you were; my mother said only an idiot would do such a thing. It was the closest they ever came to agreeing on anything."

"Oh, they agreed we shouldn't get married." Mike laughed. "I remember you sneaking your clothes out, piece by piece, so they wouldn't suspect that we were going to elope. And I remember . . ."

Jason slowed his Jeep as he neared Val's office. It was after five, but he hoped to catch her before she left. He glanced toward the parking lot and saw her car.

Then he saw her.

She was standing near the end of the building, talking to a man. The guy reminded him of a younger version of Martin Sheen, and as far as Jason was concerned, he was standing far too close to Val.

Slowing his Jeep to a crawl, Jason watched. The guy was laughing . . . and so was Val.

For a moment he stared at the two of them, hating the feelings tearing at his insides. Then he realized who the guy was, that he'd seen pictures of him in a photo album Val had once brought to the haunted house.

Stepping on the gas, Jason sped on by.

As Val shook her head at another memory of her high school days, she noticed Jason's Jeep. She started to wave, but it was too late. He was past and gone, heading out of town.

He had to have seen her. She was sure of it.

Numbly she stared after the blur of blue metal, half expecting, half hoping to see brake lights come on. Not until the Jeep was out of sight did it register that Mike was still talking.

"Did you hear a word I said?" he asked.

"I'm sorry," she heard herself say, her mind still on Jason. Where was he going? Why hadn't he stopped?

Had he seen Mike?

He had to have.

"Hey, I'm talking to you!" Mike said, raising his voice.

He had her complete attention now, and her irritation. Stiffening her spine, she lifted her chin and looked him straight in the eyes. "And where is this talk going? Yes, I remember the things we did when we were young and in love. And yes, it was fun. But that was a lifetime ago, Mike. I also remember miserable times, times when you'd verbally run me down and hit me. Times I had to hide from you. I remember you showing up three years ago and giving me this same spiel about how you'd changed. And worst of all, I remember believing you."

"This time is different," he argued.

"Yes, it is," she agreed calmly. "This time I don't care."

"You can't mean that." She could tell he didn't believe her.

"Oh, but I do. It's over, Mike."

As quickly as a summer storm formed, Mike's expression changed from smiling to glaring. "It's this guy you're seeing, isn't it? I've heard about him. Some movie star."

"He's a special effects man," Val corrected him, disturbed that Mike even knew about Jason. "But he's not the problem, it's you. You're the one who killed what we had."

"I heard *he* killed his wife."

"Well, you heard wrong."

"You sure about that?"

"I know Jason wouldn't hurt anyone." She turned and started toward her car.

"I'm the only man for you," Mike said, grabbing her arm. "And I'm not leaving until you realize that."

Old fears surfaced the moment she felt his fingers tighten on her arm, but she didn't cower. Staying cool, she looked back at him. "Either let me go, or I scream. And if you harass me, I'll call the sheriff."

He did let her go, glaring at her. He'd never been a good loser, she remembered. Then he smiled. "I know where you live . . . where he lives."

The threat was obvious. She took a step back. "If you ever—"

He merely smiled. "You'd better get going or you'll be late for your date."

She wanted to run, but forced herself to walk to her car. She wanted away from him, away from the coldness in his eyes and the memories of the pain he could inflict. Her entire body shaking, she threw her car into reverse, backed up, then switched to drive and gunned the motor. Her tires were spinning gravel when she left the parking lot, and she hoped some of it hit Mike.

Why had he come back?

Why wouldn't he leave her alone?

She drove straight to the Clifford house. She knew Jason wasn't there; he hadn't come back through town. Still, he was so much a part of the house, being in it made her feel closer to him. She mumbled greetings to the two women working on the webbing that would hang in the passageway, and headed for the telephone.

She knew Sheriff Maxwell fairly well. He'd spoken to the WIN group a couple of times, could always be depended on for a donation to the safe house, and always brought his kids to the haunted house on Halloween. It didn't take him long to agree to have a deputy keep on eye on her house and Jason's.

A few others showed up to work. Two of the members' husbands were virtually rebuilding the shed out back, keeping the old look, but ensuring its structural soundness and turning it into a souvenir shop; and an electrician from Downieville was down in the passageway, doing the necessary wiring. At six o'clock Val ordered two large pizzas and had them delivered. After a half-hour break everyone went back to work.

Val felt safe with so many people around. What bothered her was Jason's absence. Every hour, she called his place, letting the phone ring until the sound echoed through her head. She had asked the others if they knew where he'd been going or when he would be back. No one seemed to know anything.

At ten o'clock people began to leave, and Val knew she couldn't stay in the house all night. She asked the electrician to stick around while she locked up, and she made sure she drove off before he did.

If Mike was around, she didn't see him.

At her place she locked her door as soon as she was inside, turned on every light, checked every closet, behind every door, and under her bed. Even when she was sure Mike wasn't in the house, she couldn't get rid of the sick feeling in the pit of her stomach or keep her nerves from jumping every time a car slowed as it passed her house.

When one car stopped, her heart caught in her throat. Only when she saw it was Dick Asher, the town's deputy, did she relax at all. "All okay?" he asked when she opened her door.

"So far," she said.

"I haven't seen anyone in town or around here that fits the description you gave, and I've been by your place and McLain's several times tonight. He's not home, you know?"

"I know, and I appreciate what you're doing. Knowing my ex, Mike's probably at Rosie's getting drunk." And would show up in the middle of the night, yelling and swearing. That's the way it had been in the past.

"Well, if you have any problems, just call." The deputy patted the beeper on his belt. "I'll be here in a minute." He tipped his hat and stepped back.

She locked the door again and watched him drive away, then she tried Jason's number again.

It was after midnight when she finally fell asleep, but even then it wasn't a sound sleep. The next morning she didn't feel rested. Squinting at the glare from the sunlight breaking through the pines, she groaned at the thought of driving to Grass Valley. She'd be lucky to keep her own eyes open, much less examine anyone else's eyes.

She was just about to pour herself a cup of coffee when her telephone rang. Startled, she stared at it for a moment, not moving until the second ring. Then she answered it cautiously. Only when she heard Jason's voice did she release the breath she'd been holding.

"You heading down below today?" he asked.

"As usual." She wanted to ask him where he'd been, why he hadn't stopped when he saw her with Mike. She didn't. Instead, she asked what he was doing that day.

"Not sure," he answered.

"Are you working on the house?"

"Why?"

"Just curious." Even through the telephone, she could feel the strain between them. His voice was too even, his answers too short. She knew what was wrong and decided to face it. "I saw you yesterday, when I was talking to my ex-husband. Why didn't you stop?"

"The way you were laughing, I didn't think you'd want me to."

There was no missing the accusation in his tone. "You thought wrong. I was laughing at some good memories, but I haven't forgotten the bad ones. It's over between Mike and me. I wasn't even tempted this time."

"You're sure?" he asked, not sounding convinced.

"I'm sure." How could she want Mike after getting to know Jason? "Only I'm not sure Mike's accepted that. He knows about you and me, Jason. I'm worried that he might do something stupid. I even called the sheriff last night and asked him to keep an eye on your place and mine."

"So that's why he went by this morning."

"Either he or his deputy go by here about once every half hour."

"That often." He seemed to consider the information, then changed the subject. "Will you be working on the house tonight?"

As tired as she was, she knew she should go to bed early, but she wanted to see Jason. He still didn't sound quite like himself. "Why?"

"I need to get that arm on our 'lady-in-mourning' working and the laser projectors set up for Clifford's ghost. I could use your help."

"Then I'll be there."

ELEVEN

It was the middle of the afternoon, but there was little traffic on the road. The sheriff's car had gone by five minutes earlier, and if the man stuck to his routine, he wouldn't be back for another twenty-five minutes. Ample time to do what was needed without being spotted. Only the Steller's jay in the white oak behind the garage could see anything, and no one would give heed to its warning.

The propane gas tank behind the house was well out of view. It wasn't difficult to attach the small amount of plastic and the timer on the back side. Even if someone did walk by, it wouldn't be noticeable. No one would suspect the explosion wasn't an accident—a gas leak suddenly ignited. Come midnight, the town of Slaterville was going to hear a big bang.

And then it would be over.

That night, at the haunted house, Val worked with Jason on the mannequin they had named "the lady-in-mourning," helping him adjust the tension in her arm so it would move freely. There was ample tension in Val. She wanted to be alone with Jason so they could talk. He'd said so little since she'd arrived, only glancing her way now and then, and she knew all was not well.

It wasn't until the last volunteer had said good night and walked out the door that Val dared bring up the subject of Mike. "You're upset, aren't you?"

Jason looked up from the wires he was connecting. "About what?"

"Mike."

"Why should I be upset?"

"Good question. You shouldn't be, but you're certainly acting as if you were."

"I'm busy." He looked back at the wires. "I want to get this done tonight."

"So seeing me with Mike didn't bother you at all?"

A shrug was all she got.

"All right, then," she said, changing tactics, "may I ask where you were last night?"

Again he glanced up. "How do you know I wasn't home?"

"I called your place . . . several times."

"I had a problem to deal with."

"Would this problem have had anything to do with Mike being in town?"

Jason straightened, a frown darkening his expression. "What do you want me to say, Val? That I was jealous as hell, that I hated seeing you with him—seeing you laughing?"

She didn't back away, but lifted her chin and looked him straight in the eyes. "If that's how you felt, yes."

"Well, that's how I felt. But I got over it. So can we drop this subject now?"

"I guess." It was clear he wasn't going to talk about it. Only she couldn't completely drop the subject. "I half expected to find Mike hanging around my house when I got back this evening. Did you see him at all today?"

"No. Disappointed that he didn't show up?"

"Of course not." Confused better described her feelings. "It's just that he's usually more persistent, more of a pest. That's why I moved up here and didn't let anyone know where I was. He's not a man who takes no for an answer."

"Maybe he finally realized it's over between the two of you. You did tell him it was, didn't you?"

"Yes." She just hadn't expected him to believe her.

"What if I weren't around?" Jason asked, again frowning. "Would you want him back then?"

"That would be like asking for a case of the flu to return." As it was, she felt ill. "What do you mean, if you weren't around? You're not still thinking of leaving, are you?"

He looked back at the wires. "I think I should."

"Why?" It made no sense to her. "Why leave a place where people have grown to know and like you, to trust you? Why hide if you're innocent?"

Jason knew he couldn't explain his fears. "You don't understand. Val, my innocence is the question. Will always be the question."

"I do understand," she said firmly, and he looked up at her. In the clear blue of her eyes he saw the certainty and faith he wished he could find.

"I know you're haunted by your wife's death," she

went on, gently. "That not knowing who did it or why is driving you crazy. And I know that it hurts that your mother believes you killed your brother. If I could prove to you that you didn't do it, I would. How I wish I could. But until then, you just have to believe me. I know there's no monster inside of you."

"There was a green-eyed monster yesterday," he confessed.

"So?" She stepped in front of him. "Jason, I get jealous when I see you talking to Julia or that cute little redhead, Bernice, and that scares me. I didn't ever again want to care so much for a man that I made myself vulnerable. But with you, I am."

"You don't need to be jealous of Julia or Bernice," he said, touching the side of her face. Not once had he been tempted by those two volunteers, even though each woman had made it clear she was available.

"And you don't need to be jealous of Jim or Mike," Val said. "But I'm glad you felt that way, because it tells me you care."

"Care?" That she even questioned his feelings surprised him. "Woman, I'm sleeping with you."

She shrugged and managed a smile. "That doesn't mean you . . . you . . ."

When she didn't finish, he finished for her. "Love you?"

He saw the uncertainty in her eyes and knew she would have looked away if he hadn't stopped her. As it was, she lowered her lids, chestnut lashes brushing over the pink in her cheeks, and she barely spoke above a whisper. "Do you?"

"Yes," he said. Not that he'd wanted to love her or thought it was wise. It simply had happened. "I think I fell in love with you the first day you walked into my house."

Her eyes seemed darker when she lifted her lids, her expression more relaxed. For a moment she stared at his face, then she sighed. "I think I fell in love with you the first time I saw your picture in the papers."

"Proclaiming me a murderer." It was back to that, he thought, would always come back to that. "Val, how do you know I'm not? You say there's no monster in me, but how can we prove I don't have some sort of split personality . . . that I don't do these terrible things and never remember them?"

"I just know," she said, hugging him. "Split personalities don't just come out once every few years and stay dormant the rest of the time."

"Are you sure there couldn't be one that just comes out when a person gets jealous?"

"You've been jealous twice with me," she said. "Nothing's happened."

"Yet."

She pulled back, frowning. "What are you trying to do, torture me? Do you want me spending the rest of my life wondering when something will happen?"

"No," he admitted, tired of even thinking about the future. He'd spent too many hours that day thinking about it, debating between staying in Slaterville and leaving. He still hadn't decided, but he knew what he wanted now. "Come home with me," he said, bringing her back into his embrace. "Make love with me all night long."

She snuggled against him. "More torture."

"The worst kind." He chuckled into her curls.

"I'm not sure what kind of a lover I'd be tonight. I didn't get much sleep last night."

"Nor did I." He kissed her forehead. "Just don't snore while we're doing it."

"I don't snore," she said, and pulled back, grabbing his hand. "Let's go."

They hurried to turn off the lights and lock up. Val decided to leave her car at the haunted house and ride with Jason. Sitting back in the passenger's seat, she played his words through her memory. He loved her. He'd said it. All those nights when she'd wondered— sometimes sure he did, other times questioning her sanity—had been wasted energy.

He was a man who'd known Hollywood beauties, who'd been married to an actress. He could have any woman in Slaterville. But *he* loved *her*.

Turning her head, she looked at him. His was a profile chiseled in granite—darkness and shadows, strength and intensity. He was afraid of hurting her physically; she knew her greatest danger was what he could do to her emotionally.

Still watching him, she felt her lids grow heavy and fought back a yawn. He glanced her way and chuckled. "You are tired, aren't you? Maybe I should just drop you off at your house, let you get some sleep."

Quickly she straightened in her seat and forced her eyes wide open. "Don't you dare."

"I cheated this afternoon," he said. "I got a nap. In fact, it was weird. I think I walked in my sleep. When I woke up, I had my jeans on, but I'd swear I took them off before lying down."

"That is weird, or maybe you were so tired you just

thought you took them off." She'd been that tired before.

He didn't slow as he passed her place, and she relaxed back against the seat. The clock on the dash read eleven forty-five. Nearly midnight. Another mile up the hill and they'd be at his place. It was strange, but she felt as though she were going home.

He parked in front of his garage, and she didn't wait for him to come around and let her out. Together they walked to his side door. In the woods behind the house, crickets sang while a breeze whispered through the treetops. There was just a slight nip to the air, a warning that summer would soon be over.

He followed her inside, but didn't close the door. Instead, he stopped and looked back at his car. "Have you ever had a feeling that you've forgotten something?" he asked, frowning.

"Like?"

"I don't know." He shook his head, still staring out the doorway. "Like maybe something back at the house."

"We shut off the lights and locked up."

"But I don't remember turning off the motor for the mannequin." He glanced her way. "Do you mind if I run back and check on it? After all the problems I've had getting it to work, I don't want it running all night. And I certainly wouldn't want it overheating and starting a fire."

A fire was the last thing they needed. "Go ahead."

"You stay here." He checked the clock in his kitchen. "I'll be back before midnight."

Val watched him back out of the driveway and head down the hill, then she closed the door and looked around his kitchen. One thing she'd learned about Jason, he'd never be awarded a Housekeeper of the Year award. The man was a slob. Leftovers of a frozen dinner sat on his table, while his sink was filled with dirty dishes.

She put some hot water on the stove to heat for instant coffee, but she didn't have the energy to tackle the dishes. Wandering into his living room, she started for his sofa, then stopped herself. As tired as she was, if she sat down, she'd probably fall asleep. So she kept moving.

On one wall of the room he'd taped the storyboard he'd brought to her house back in April. If the tape marred the paint on the walls, he didn't seem to care. On his coffee table was a model of the gambling scene, each miniature figure almost an exact duplicate of what now was full-size in the game room. His creativity amazed her.

Moving on, she came to the three enameled Chinese puzzle boxes he'd placed on the fireplace mantel. Val stroked the largest box. Though they'd belonged to his wife, she was glad he'd brought them out and put them on display. They were really quite fascinating, and just the other night they'd decided to open the largest one. But then they'd gotten distracted.

How easily they ended up in his bedroom.

Curious, she wandered on into that room. The moment she stepped through the doorway, she smiled. As she'd expected, his bed wasn't made. It never was.

"You *are* a slob, Jason McLain," she said aloud, and knew he'd never change. If they ever got married, she'd have to live with it.

Marriage. She let the idea roll over in her head.

She'd thought of the possibility before, but only briefly, never truly believing it might happen. And it never would if she couldn't convince him he wasn't a murderer. She knew that for certain.

On the corner of his dresser stood his three Oscars. She'd wanted him to put them in his living room, too, to show them off. He'd said no, that he'd never felt he really deserved them. It was teamwork, he'd said, that had won him each one, and putting them out would be like ignoring the other people on the team.

From the work they'd done on the haunted house, Val understood what he meant by teamwork. She also knew the house would have been nothing without him, that a team needed a leader. She had a feeling he deserved each of the Oscars.

She heard a noise outside and walked over to the window to look out. From the light of the moon, she could see a corner of Jason's propane tank and the shadows of trees across his backyard. Pushing up the window, she listened.

The crickets continued to sing and a mosquito buzzed close to the screen, but she heard nothing more. "Anyone out there?" she called, not expecting an answer.

But she did hear something, a rattle, like the lid of a garbage can.

She dashed back to the kitchen and opened the side door. The outside light illuminated the walkway between his house and the garage. Stepping out, she looked toward the backyard. The white oak behind the garage created a dark silhouette against the inky sky; the woods farther back were a black backdrop.

"Mike?" she called.

She knew it was stupid to leave the house. She was doing it again, just like those idiotic women in the spooky movies who left the sanctuary of their houses and walked right into danger. Yet Val couldn't stop herself from taking a few steps away from the door toward the back of the house. She needed to know for certain that it was Mike before she made a real fool of herself and called the sheriff. And she was close enough, she was sure, that she could dash back inside and lock the door before anyone—Mike in particular—could get her. She was safe.

A moment later she realized she was wrong.

Her mistake was where she was looking. She'd been checking at eye level, expecting to see a man. It wasn't until she glanced down that she understood what had made the noise . . . and the danger she was in.

His body was solid black, but there was no mistaking the white stripe on his tail, and somehow he'd gotten between her and the house already. Running no longer seemed a good idea to Val, not the way the skunk's tail was raised.

"Nice skunky," she said quietly, inching back a step. "What a surprise to meet you."

He paused and looked at her.

"Oh, don't let me stop you," she crooned. "You can keep right on going."

The skunk took a step toward her, and she tensed, stepping back again and slightly to the side.

"Ah, do you have any particular place in mind that you were headed?" she asked, half hoping Jason would come home and half hoping he wouldn't. She wasn't sure what the arrival of his car might do. Eau de skunk wasn't exactly the scent she preferred.

Again the skunk stopped and again Val stepped back. "You just stay where you are, Mr. Le Peu," she said, working her way farther from the house. "*Mi casa es su casa.* Or in this case, Jason's house is yours."

The skunk seemed to understand and turned back toward Jason's side door.

"Hey, whoa!" she called after it, not moving herself. "I wasn't serious. You can't go in there."

Again the skunk stopped.

"It's a nice night out," she said. "Why go into a stuffy old house? Stay out here. Take a walk. Maybe disappear into those woods back there."

Instead, he continued walking toward the side door.

"Damn!" she muttered, wondering how she and Jason would get a skunk out of his house. If only she'd closed that door. No, if only she'd stayed inside. She certainly hadn't learned anything from those movies.

Then a miracle occurred. The skunk veered away from the doorway and started toward Jason's front yard.

With a sigh Val headed back toward the house.

Jason again locked the door to the haunted house and started for his car. Why he'd thought he'd left the motor running on the mannequin, he didn't know. It was off. Everything in the house was turned off and locked up. Maybe he was more tired than he thought. His brain wasn't functioning anymore.

In his Jeep he checked the time. One minute to midnight. He wasn't going to get back when he'd promised. Not that it probably mattered. As tired as Val had looked, she was undoubtedly asleep by now. And that wouldn't bother him. Though he loved making love with her, tonight he mainly wanted her with him, sleeping beside him.

Driving toward his house, he grimaced, remembering the condition he'd left his bed in. He should have made it, should have changed the linens. Karen always used to have the maid change their linens once a week and always had the bed made. What he needed was a maid.

Or a wife.

No, he told himself. He could not let himself think of marrying Val. It was bad enough that he'd told her he loved her. There could be no future for them, not with so many unanswered questions hanging over his head. What he should do was leave Slaterville, get out of her life.

He'd just passed her house when a dull thud reverberated through the night. He knew the sound. For two years he'd trained as a prop maker, then for six months had learned the use of explosives. He'd even taken the Class 3 state-approved course in explosives, and had passed the exam, all eighty pages of it. He knew how to create explosions, large and small, how to blow up cars and buildings, and how to give the directors what they wanted and the audiences a thrill.

The thud hit like a kick to his gut, a wave of nausea sweeping over him. Without knowing why, he knew the explosion had been at his place.

His house, with Val inside. With Val sleeping.

Stepping on the gas, he sped up the hill, swerving around the curves, only barely aware of people coming out of their houses, still in their nightclothes, all staring up the hill. Even the sounds of the sirens starting up down below barely penetrated his concentration. All he knew was he had to get to her.

There was always a chance, a prayer of a chance.

And then he saw his house, its windows blown out, the back half gone. Flames leaped to the sky, and he knew it was too late for prayers. No one inside could have survived that blast.

Stopping his Jeep, he sagged against the steering wheel.

TWELVE

A fire truck went by Jason's Jeep, the blare of the siren dying out as it pulled up in front of the burning house. Numbly Jason lifted his head to watch three men climb off the back of the truck and two get out of the cab. He'd seen the scene before—on movie sets. In those shots, he'd rigged the explosions, he'd been in control.

He wasn't in control now, and these men were not actors.

Through eyes blurred with tears, he merely watched, knowing that saving what remained of the house wasn't important. Nothing inside had meant anything. Nothing except the one thing they wouldn't be able to save. The way the windows were blown out, he knew no one in the house could have survived.

Once again closing his eyes, he tried to block out the vision of his house exploding, of everything inside exploding. He wanted it to be a gag. He wanted to open his eyes and see everything as he'd left it—windows intact, walls in place, and Val standing in the doorway, smiling. Slowly he opened his eyes again and stared at the raging fire.

Val was not there.

Hypnotically he gazed out his window, unable to move or even cry out his anguish. Deep inside, an emptiness engulfed him, sucking away the tendrils of sanity. Too many times this had happened to him. Too many times he had lost someone he loved.

A movement at the edge of the road caught his attention. He glanced that way and sucked in a breath, afraid to believe what he thought he saw.

Like a zombie in a trance, Val walked to the middle of the road, staring at the burning house. Her hair was tousled, her body covered with dirt and pine needles, and in her arms she carried something, cradling it like a child. She stopped next to the fire truck, her body swaying slightly, never taking her eyes from the burning house.

Jason was by her side in a second, holding her, and the moment he put his arms around her and felt her tremble, he knew she was real. "Oh my God, Val," he gasped, ignoring the dirt in her hair as he buried his face in her curls. "You're alive."

"I . . . it . . ." She didn't look at him but at the house, her glazed eyes reflecting the flames.

"I thought you were in there," he said, releasing his hold and stepping back to look at her. That she was standing in front of him—alive—seemed unreal.

"I came outside," she said shakily. "I heard a noise." She looked down at the small, limp black body cradled in her arms.

Jason recognized the oddly marked skunk. It wasn't moving. "Freddy?"

Val repeated the name, her expression confused.

"The skunk you have there." Jason touched the small animal. It didn't move. "He belongs to the Vernons. Jeff and Tonya. They live down the hill. He's their pet, and once in a while he'll get loose and come up to visit. The first time I saw him was a panic."

"I panicked," Val said, her gaze now focused on the animal, her voice distant. "I almost went back inside. And I would have, but he turned around and started coming straight for me. I kept backing up. And then . . ."

She looked at what was left of his house. "It exploded, Jason. One minute I was on my feet, the next I was on the ground across the road." Again she glanced down at the skunk. "If I'd known he was someone's pet . . ."

She might not have kept backing up, Jason thought, might have been closer to the house when the explosion occurred. Might not be alive.

Another fire truck pulled up in front of the first, then an ambulance. People were beginning to arrive, some driving, some running up the hill. "There are the Vernons." Jason pointed toward a young couple nearing the spot where he'd parked his Jeep. "Let's give them Freddy, then get you checked by a doctor."

"I don't need a doctor. I'm fine, really," Val said. "A little shaken up, maybe. That's all."

Jason didn't argue, he simply guided her toward the Vernons. Val, he was certain, was in shock. She didn't feel too steady on her feet, and she was still shaking. He held her close while she explained to the Vernons how their skunk had lured her out of the house and to safety.

"I'm so sorry," she said, handing the limp body to Jeff Vernon.

He took the skunk from her, his sigh deep as he caressed the animal's soft fur. Then he frowned, moved his hand under the skunk's foreleg, and looked up. "He's not dead. I feel a heartbeat."

"But I thought . . ." Val reached forward at the same time Tonya Vernon did. They both felt the skunk's chest, and Val glanced back at Jason. "He's right."

"Maybe the blast knocked him out," Tonya said, stroking the little animal, tears running down her cheeks. "Maybe he's just stunned."

"Maybe," Jason agreed. It had been a night of miracles. Why not one more?

To everyone's relief, the fire was quickly extinguished, the danger of it spreading to the surrounding trees and undergrowth eliminated. Smoke changed to steam, the smoldering wood hissing as water hit it. Turning away from the Vernons, Val stared at what remained of Jason's house. "It's gone," she said sadly.

She was nearly right. His garage, two bedrooms, kitchen, and bathroom were no more than charred timbers, and all that remained of the living room and dining area was a shell. What hadn't been blown to pieces was now water soaked and sooty.

It didn't matter to him. He had what was important. He gave Val a squeeze, needing to reassure himself that she was truly there.

She winced slightly, and he loosened his hold. "Let's get you looked at."

"Really, I'm fine," she said again, but went with him to the ambulance, where a paramedic stood waiting.

Except for the sheriff's department, a fire chief, and

a paramedic, Slaterville's emergency services were made up of volunteers. A few of the men and women who'd come to fight the fire had also helped on the haunted house. Everyone knew Jason at least by reputation.

The fire out, they put away the hoses and cleaned up, then stopped by to share their condolences. While the paramedic checked Val and Sheriff Maxwell strung a yellow crime tape around the boundaries of Jason's property, Captain Hargus, the fire chief, questioned both of them. Jason had no idea what would have caused the explosion.

Val did.

"I put some water on for coffee," she said. "Then later I went outside and left the door open. A draft could have blown out the flame."

And a spark could have ignited the gas, Jason thought.

"As long as you're safe, I don't care what happened," he said. "Things don't matter. People do."

Looking at the charred remains of the house, Val felt ill. Jason could say what he wanted about possessions meaning nothing, but she knew there were things in that house that he treasured. Things that couldn't be replaced, like his Oscars, his late wife's puzzle boxes, and photos. "I'm so sorry," she said, and felt the tears well in her eyes.

"Don't be sorry about anything," he told her. "I'm just glad you're all right. She is all right, isn't she?" he asked the paramedic.

"Except for a few scrapes and bruises, and being a little shaken up, she's fine," the man said, closing his bag. "It's a miracle." He gave her shoulder an affectionate squeeze. "Consider yourself one very lucky lady."

"I do."

"Sheriff Maxwell and I will be doing a complete investigation," Captain Hargus told Jason. "Nothing is to be touched until we're finished. We'll let you know when we're done. Where will you be staying?"

Val answered for Jason. "He'll be at my place."

She thought he might object, but he didn't. He said nothing as he walked her back to his Jeep. The Vernons were still standing there, now grinning.

"Look," Jeff said, holding up their skunk for them to see. Freddy blinked at them with glazed eyes, then wiggled in Jeff's hands, struggling to get back to a more secure position against the man's chest and shirt.

"A little dazed, I'd say," Jason said. "But definitely alive."

Jeff nodded. "Definitely."

Val gently stroked the skunk, so glad she hadn't known how tame the animal was. "I guess we both lucked out."

The Vernons refused their offer of a ride back to their place, saying being in a car might upset Freddy right now and it wasn't far to walk. Val still expected Jason to refuse her offer. She supposed that was why she talked all the way down the hill. If he couldn't get a word in edgewise, how could he refuse to stay with her?

When he pulled into her drive and didn't get out after stopping, she knew she hadn't talked enough and his objections were coming. "I shouldn't stay with you," he said. "There's really going to be talk now."

"It's too late to worry about that," she reminded him. "Captain Hargus thinks you'll be here, so you might as well be."

Jason hesitated a moment longer, then nodded and got out.

She didn't think about how she looked, not until she stood in front of the mirror in the bathroom. Then she saw the dirt and pine needles that clung to her hair and clothes, and how pale her face was, where it wasn't smudged with grit. "I'm going to take a shower," she called to Jason.

He was there with a towel when she stepped out of the shower, then he wrapped her in her terry cloth bathrobe, cinching the sash tight around her waist. He made her take two aspirins and drink some hot milk. Leading her to her bed, he told her to get some sleep.

She didn't want to sleep.

She couldn't stop talking. Like a spring too tightly wound, she had to let it out. "I was in your bedroom when I heard a noise outside. I thought it was Mike. It was stupid to go outside and leave that door open. I never thought about the stove. It's all Mike's fault. If he hadn't shown up the other day, I wouldn't have thought it was him." She looked up at Jason. "It's all my fault."

"It's no one's fault," he insisted.

"But if I'd—"

His mouth covering hers silenced her arguments. Explosions and guilt were forgotten, the taste of life more compelling. Wrapping her arms around his waist, she held on to the reality of the moment. She was alive. He was alive. And they had each other.

Her body pressed against his, she could feel his growing arousal through his shorts. The bulky thickness of her robe frustrated her, and she waited for him to release the sash. To her surprise, he released her instead and stepped back. "You need to sleep."

"I don't want to sleep," she said. Life was too precious to waste on sleep. Closing the space between them, she put her hands on his waist, teasingly slipping her fingers beneath the waistband of his shorts.

She heard him suck in a breath and felt his body tense. Nevertheless, he again stepped back. "You've had a shock. You were thrown across the road. The paramedic said your body's going to be bruised and hurting tomorrow. You need your rest."

"I don't hurt now," she said, though her hips and shoulders, where she'd landed on the hard ground, were beginning to ache. "What I need is you, Jason."

Slowly she undid the sash herself, letting the robe fall loose and giving him a tempting view of her body. His gaze dropped to her breasts, then lower. With a groan, he gave in.

There was something desperate in the way they came together, the joining of their bodies a joining of their souls. She felt his fear while he eased hers. To know how close she'd come to death was frightening. But to know how much he cared gave her strength.

She'd thought herself too overwrought to sleep, but when they were finished and he cradled her in his arms, sleep came like a blessing. It was seven A.M. when her alarm by the bed went off. Groaning, she reached over and silenced it. Every muscle in her body ached. Lying back, she stared at the ceiling.

The birds outside her windows were singing their delight with the morning. Everything that had happened the night before seemed like a dream, yet her body was proclaiming its reality. Muscles she'd never known she had screamed for relief. Going into her office and looking into patients' eyes did not sound appealing.

Beside her, one leg draped over hers, lay Jason, his breathing deep and peaceful. She tried to extricate her leg without waking him or moaning, but before she eased herself out of bed, he caught her hand. "Where are you going?"

"To call Ginger and tell her I won't be in today."

"Good idea. You should rest." He released her hand, but his gaze skimmed over her naked body. "How do you feel?"

"Like King Kong jumped up and down on me."

"You may have broken something." He sat up, the rumpled sheet falling down to his hips, exposing the dark hairs that covered his chest and abdomen. "You should see a doctor today."

The outline of his hips and legs was defined beneath the sheet, and she could see he was partially aroused. The memory of how he'd felt inside of her only a few hours earlier sent a warmth to the depth of her, and she knew her injuries weren't that serious. "Nothing's broken. What I need is bed rest," she said. "Maybe a massage . . . and a little light exercise. Something where I can lie on my back." She grinned seductively. "Interested?"

Concern showed in his eyes as he studied her face, then he smiled. "Go make your call, then I'll give you that massage."

It was after ten and they were making love when the telephone rang. Jason hesitated, but Val shook her head. "Let the answering machine take the message."

A little while later Jason showered, then pulled on the same shirt and shorts he'd worn the day before. One thing he knew, he'd have to buy some new clothes.

Val waited until they were finished with breakfast before telling him what the message had been. "I need to go into my office after all," she said. "Minor emergency. The Fisher girl's eyes are all red. Could be her contacts or it could be a virus, but I need to look at them. It shouldn't take me more than an hour."

"I'll drive you down," he said, "then go look at what's left of my place. Afterward I'll pick you up, and we can get your car."

She hung her head. "I'm so sorry about your house, Jason."

"I told you. Don't worry about it." He forced a laugh. "The place needed a good cleaning."

"I'll help you. Maybe more survived than we think."

"You survived. That's all that's important."

An hour later Jason dropped her off at her office. "I'll be back soon," he promised. "I'm just going to take a quick look around. That's all."

To Jason's surprise, Captain Hargus was at the remains of his house, digging through the rubble. He looked Jason's way and frowned. And then, from behind a standing wall, Sheriff Maxwell stepped out.

When an hour passed and Jason didn't show up, Val made excuses for him. "He's probably lost track of the time," she told Ginger. "Got looking around and forgot everything else. I'll do some paperwork until he gets here."

When two hours passed and he still hadn't shown

up, she knew something was wrong. "Drive me to my car," she said to Ginger. "I'm going to see what's up."

They were just about to leave her office when Debbie came through the door. "He's in jail," she said breathlessly. "I just found out."

"Jason?" Val asked, feeling a sick knot form in her stomach.

Debbie nodded. "The sheriff arrested him an hour or so ago."

"For what?" Val and Ginger asked at the same time.

"For trying to kill you. I told you he was a murderer, that he killed his wife. All this nice guy stuff, it was all a front."

"He tried to kill you?" Ginger asked, looking at Val.

Val shook her head. "No. I caused the explosion. I'm the one who turned on the stove and caused the gas leak. Why would the sheriff arrest him?"

"It wasn't a gas leak that caused the explosion," Debbie said. "It was a bomb. And not just some simple pipe bomb, but one like they use in those espionage movies. Sheriff Maxwell said it was made of plastic explosives and a timer, and it was a good thing that gas tank was almost empty, or you wouldn't have simply been thrown across the road. Both Captain Hargus and the sheriff were there when Jason came back to the scene of the crime."

"Jason didn't go back to the scene of the crime," Val said, too upset by what she was hearing to know what to think. "He went back to look things over, clean up."

"To get rid of the evidence probably. Only he was too late. Captain Hargus found bits and pieces of the bomb. The sheriff's already sent some of it down to

Sacramento to have it analyzed. He thinks they can tell who sold it from the threads in it, or something like that. Even if Jason doesn't confess, they've got him."

"Assuming he bought it," Val pointed out. "When would he have had a chance to buy it?"

"One of those trips he made getting supplies for the haunted house," Debbie said smugly, then frowned. "What I don't understand is why he tried to kill you, Val. I thought you two were getting along great."

"We were . . . are." Val quickly corrected herself. "He did not plant that bomb." But she had a good idea who had, and she needed to tell the sheriff.

It took her less than five minutes to walk to the sheriff's office. "Sheriff Maxwell, you're holding an innocent man," she said as she stepped into his office.

He looked up from the sheet of paper on his desk, then glanced at the closest of the two cells behind him. Jason had already stood and come to the bars, grabbing two. He was looking straight at her. "Val, this is for the best," he called to her.

She ignored him, going to the sheriff's desk. "The man you should have in there is my ex-husband. He's the one who planted that bomb. He said he'd get Jason, and he tried."

Sheriff Maxwell glanced back at Jason. "You want to tell her why it wasn't her ex or shall I?"

Val frowned, looking at Jason. He took in a deep breath, straightening. "Mike is in Sacramento, Val. I drove him there myself Wednesday night. After I saw the two of you talking outside your office, I circled around and came back. I heard his threats to you. After you left, we had a little talk."

"What kind of a talk?" she asked cautiously.

Jason smiled slightly. "A persuasive talk. I convinced him he wasn't welcome in Slaterville."

"You beat him up?"

"No . . . but I convinced him he was in over his head and would be a lot healthier if he stayed away from you."

"And then you drove him to Sacramento?"

Jason nodded. "I had to. The guy didn't have a car. He'd hitchhiked up."

"He could have come back," she argued, looking at the sheriff again. "Just because Jason made a few threats and drove Mike to Sacramento doesn't mean Mike took him seriously and stayed there."

"I checked," the sheriff said. "Your ex has an airtight alibi. He was with his probation officer from the time Jason dropped him off until six o'clock last night."

"He could have set the bomb before he came to my office."

Sheriff Maxwell shook his head. "This one used a twelve-hour clock. If he'd set it the day before, the bomb would have gone off before it did."

"Why?" she asked, her gaze shifting to Jason. "Why would you want to kill me?"

"Jealousy," Jason answered calmly. "I guess I can't control it."

She walked over to where he stood, frustrated by the bars separating them. She wanted to shake some sense into him. "I don't believe that, just like I don't believe you killed your wife."

"Well, maybe you'd better. Maybe you're a lot safer with me in here."

"What you're saying is crazy," she insisted, gripping his hands. And if there was one thing she knew, Jason McLain was not a crazy man.

He glanced past her at the sheriff, then sighed and lowered his voice. "I love you, Val. I would never knowingly do anything to hurt you, you have to believe that. But it's got to be me who set that bomb. Who else would it be?"

"Someone who wants to kill you."

"And who around here wants to kill me?"

She wished she knew. That had to be the answer, only everyone around Slaterville seemed to like Jason. Oh, there were some who still had their suspicions and who, like Debbie, would probably now readily proclaim they'd always thought him a murderer. And some, she suspected, were afraid of him. But as far as she knew, no one hated him. Not enough to try to kill him.

"What happens now?" she asked, trying to stay calm.

Jason shook his head, and she looked back at the sheriff. "What happens now? Do I have to pay bail or something to get him out?"

"I called the judge," the sheriff said. "He'll be up here Monday. With luck, I'll have a report on that sample I sent to Sacramento." He smiled. "After that, we'll see what happens."

"You can't just keep him here all weekend . . . in this cell." She looked at Jason, her fingers tightening over his.

"It's better this way," Jason said firmly.

"It will only be until Monday, then the judge will be here," the sheriff said.

"I can't just leave you here," Val insisted.

"Yes, you can." Jason pulled his hands free from hers and stepped back, his dark brows drawing together as he looked at her. "Remember this, Val. Jealousy is a terrible emotion. It can make a man do terrible things."

THIRTEEN

Val knew about jealousy and what it could do. She'd suffered from Mike's jealousy and possessiveness. It was a disease that ate away at a person, making him crazy and turning love to cruelty. Jason was not cruel. Nor was he crazy.

After Val left the sheriff's office, Ginger drove her to her car. Standing beside it, staring at the Clifford house, Val wondered what they would do. Most of the special effects were in place, but there were glitches here and there, fine-tuning to be done. They needed Jason.

She needed Jason.

So much had happened in the last twenty-four hours, she felt dazed as she drove back to her house. She had to get Jason out of jail, but she didn't know how. As long as *he* believed he was guilty of everything that had happened, he wasn't going to be any help.

As she walked from her car to her house, she tried to think of people to call. Before she got the door open, her phone began ringing. She hurried to answer it, her "Hello" a little breathless.

When the man on the other end of the line identified himself as Bud—Bud Henke, from Los Angeles—it took her a moment to make the connection to Jason. Then she sighed with relief. "I'm so glad you called."

"Why? What's going on?" he asked. "I've been trying Jason's number all day and I keep getting a message that his phone is out of order."

A wave of weakness washed over Val, sapping her legs of strength. Sinking onto the nearest chair, she cradled the phone against her shoulder and sighed again. Her prayers had been answered. Someone who could help Jason had called. She wasn't alone. Jason had friends, friends who would help, who would make him understand he was wrong, that he couldn't have done these horrible things without knowing.

"Bud," she said shakily, her emotions raw and tears close to the surface. "Something terrible has happened."

"He's dead?"

"No. There was a bomb. His house was blown up. He blames himself, and the sheriff has arrested him."

"His house blew up?" Bud repeated. "My God, how did he survive?"

"He wasn't in it. I almost was—should have been—but I heard a noise, and it was a skunk. I was cut off from the door. I—"

She knew she was rambling. It was Bud who stopped her. "Jason wasn't in the house? Where was he at that time of night?"

"He went back to the haunted house to check if he'd turned everything off. Now he thinks he left me because he wanted me alone, that he was jealous. He thinks he does things without knowing. But he didn't do it. I just know that."

Just as she knew she couldn't stop the tears. Bud let her cry, only occasionally telling her that it was all right. She wasn't sure how long she'd cried when he asked her another question. "They're sure Jason planted the bomb?"

"Yes. And so's Jason. He's as much as confessed to it. He's sure he tried to kill me and that he did kill his wife and brother. You have to talk to him, Bud. You have to convince him he's not doing these things."

"He confessed?" There was a pause, and Val heard Bud sigh in frustration. When he spoke again, his voice sounded stronger. "Of course I'll call him and talk to him. He couldn't have done this. You and I know that. Will they let me talk to him?"

"I'm sure they will." She gave him the number of the sheriff's office. "You've seen how small Slaterville is. It's a two-cell jail, and the cells are right there in the office. They'll let him take calls." Suddenly she remembered something important. "Could you also call his lawyer? The one he had for his trial? I think he's going to need one up here."

She felt a little better after she hung up. Not quite as helpless and alone. Jason had friends in Slaterville and Hollywood. They would help, would convince him that he wasn't some sort of monster.

She went back to see him that afternoon, bringing him a change of clothes that she'd picked up at the general store and some essentials. Slaterville's jail didn't have prison uniforms. She was glad. Seeing Jason in shorts and a shirt helped her deny the reality of where he was. It was the metal bars that separated them that constantly reminded her.

They talked while the sheriff's deputy went through every item she'd brought. "I didn't put any saws or files in," she told the deputy, trying to keep the conversation light. "I'm saving them for the cake I bake."

"We've got to check," the deputy answered seriously, continuing to twist and shake every item.

She looked back at Jason. "Has Bud called?"

He shook his head. "Why would he?"

"He called me. He'd been trying to get hold of you. I told him what happened. He said he'd call."

"It doesn't matter." Jason pulled away from her touch and walked back to the pallet that was his chair and bed combined. Sitting, he propped his elbows on his knees and buried his face in his hands.

He didn't want her there. Seeing her, hearing her voice, and feeling her touch were too painful. Her eyes were red-rimmed, and he knew she'd been crying. The last thing he wanted was to make her cry.

"I told Bud to call your lawyer," she said.

Jason didn't look up, didn't say anything.

"Was I wrong in doing that? Have you already called one?"

She was worried and trying to help. She didn't understand that he didn't want help. Looking up, he glared at her. "Just stay out of this."

The words came out harsher than he'd wanted, and it hurt him to see her stiffen, yet he knew he had to do it. He had to cut all ties, drive her away.

"I'm not staying out," she said boldly, squaring her shoulders.

He knew why he loved her. Even in the face of everything, she refused to believe the worst in him. Spunky and foolish, she'd stand by his side. He couldn't let her.

"Thanks for the clothes," he said, looking her straight in the eyes. "Now go away."

She shook her head. "You can't make me leave."

"Deputy, can't a man get some rest?" Stretching out on the flat, hard board, he turned toward the stone wall that separated him from the outside world. Names and initials were scratching into the rocks, each a record of a progression of prisoners who had inhabited the cell for over a hundred years.

"Jason, don't block me out," Val pleaded from outside the cell.

He knew he had to or he would truly go crazy.

"I can't help you without your help."

He didn't want any help. He was beyond help.

She stood there, talking to him for an eternity, and it took all of his willpower not to respond, to lie in silence, staring at the wall. Finally he heard her step away, say good-bye to the deputy, and leave the office. The moment she was gone, a cold emptiness filled Jason.

She didn't come back that night.

Val went to Grass Valley on Saturday. She almost called in sick, then decided she could last half a day, and it would give her a chance to buy Jason some decent clothes for Monday, when he saw the judge.

Like a zombie, she went through the motions of giving eye exams, prescribing corrective lenses, checking contacts and glasses, and listening to patients. She explained the bruises that covered her body as briefly as possible. Before noon, however, everyone knew what had happened.

The headline on the front page of the Sacramento *Bee* was an echo of the headlines she'd first read about Jason. News of his arrest and confession for a bombing had brought back all of the old questions. A photo showed what was left of his house, the yellow police ribbon surrounding his property proclaiming it a crime scene. And Val's name was mentioned, along with her miraculous escape. The Vernons were quoted, and there was a picture of their skunk. Val was glad to see Freddy looked none the worse for his adventure.

She left the clinic at noon, did her shopping for Jason, then hit the road, anxious to return to Slaterville. To her frustration, the drive up Highway 49 took forever, one semi after another slowing her down. Snapping on the radio for diversion, she got a weather report. Rain was being predicted, and considering the giant thunderheads above, she believed the weatherman might be right.

It seemed appropriate. Her life had turned miserable. Why not the weather too?

A car was parked in front of her house. The driver got out as soon as Val stopped in her driveway. He was middle-aged and wearing wire-rimmed glasses that needed adjustment. They slipped down his nose as he hurried toward her. "Are you Valerie Wiggins?" he asked.

She stopped to face him, confused that he knew her name. She'd never seen him before, and she certainly wouldn't have done such a poor job of fitting his glasses.

"I'm doing a story," he went on, pushing the frames back up his nose. "On Jason McLain. Did he really try to kill you?"

"No," she said firmly. She would never believe he'd set that bomb.

"But you were his lover?"

The word sounded crude the way he said it. Turning away, she started for her door.

"Did you know he'd killed his wife?" he persisted, following her.

She paused before opening the door. Facing him, she made her position clear. "Jason did not kill his wife. Now, if you'll excuse me."

For a moment she thought he was going to follow her into her house. She slammed her door shut and locked it. In the two years and eleven months she'd lived in Slaterville, she'd never thought of locking her door. Now, in the last week, she'd done it twice.

The phone began ringing, and she hurried to answer it, only to hang up as soon as the caller started asking questions about Jason. Her answering machine showed eight messages. Hitting the button, she listened to each one as she kicked off her work shoes and changed to jeans and a halter top. One after another, reporters from television stations and newspapers asked her to call, each leaving his or her number. Val deleted them all. She didn't want to talk to anyone from the media.

Everything was out of focus, and she didn't know any prescription to fix it. While she slapped together a sandwich, she called the sheriff's office. Sheriff Maxwell answered the phone. She was glad to hear his voice. "Has anything changed?" she asked, unsure if she wanted a yes or a no.

"You mean other than Slaterville turning into a three-ring circus?" he returned, sounding tired.

"I had a reporter harass me right outside my house."

Peeking out her window, she could see the man's car was still there. Escaping without another confrontation was going to be difficult. "I'm going to stop by. I have some more clothes for Jason. Does he need anything else?"

She heard him ask Jason, and faintly heard Jason's responding "no." Simply hearing his voice released some of her tension.

Fifteen minutes later she was looking at him, wishing he'd look at her. The moment she'd walked through the door, he'd turned away and sat on the pallet. His back to her, he stared at the stone wall.

"You can pretend I don't exist if you want," she said, trying to ignore the stab of pain cutting through her. "But I'm not going away."

She turned toward the sheriff. "What about the things at his house? Have the reporters been picking it clean?"

"We got most everything that was salvageable yesterday. Not much was. It's all in a couple of boxes in the back room here."

"His Oscars?" she asked.

"We've got one." The sheriff stood and stretched. "And a couple of lumps that once might have been Oscars. Most of the stuff is in pretty bad shape." He looked Jason's way. "You have any objections if I give your stuff to Val?"

Jason didn't answer, merely shook his head.

"Looks like you can have it if you want."

She wanted it, and he brought out two boxes. Val glanced in each, dismayed by how little had survived the blast and fire. There was a silver picture frame with a photo of Jason with his brother and parents. Miraculously it had survived, only the glass broken. And the smallest of the Chinese puzzle boxes was intact. She saw pieces of his chess set, the remote for his television, books, and the one Oscar the sheriff had mentioned.

There were also several loose pages of what looked like part of a diary. Val picked up one.

"His wife's diary, I think," the sheriff said. "I read through some, but—"

"Diary?" Jason asked.

Val looked back to see he'd stood and come to the bars. She grabbed a couple of pages and took them to him.

He quickly read over each, then looked up. "These are recent. Written while I was in England, after she'd learned she couldn't have children. But where . . . ?"

"We found those pages mixed in with scattered pieces of enameled wood," the sheriff answered. He lifted the small Chinese puzzle box. "Wood like this, only the pieces were a lot bigger."

"The larger box," Val said, realizing it would have had ample room inside to hold a diary. "You never opened that one, Jason?"

"Never," he admitted. He glanced toward the cardboard boxes on the sheriff's desk. "Is there more?"

"Some. I didn't pick up all of the paper on the ground. Some had gotten pretty wet from the fire hoses."

Val understood the importance of the diary's pages. Karen had told Jason she'd had an affair. Where else would a woman write about her lover than in her diary? "Sheriff, can you get those pages?"

He looked at the two of them. "I don't imagine this can wait until tomorrow, can it?"

"No," they said in unison, then glanced at each other and grinned.

For the first time since she'd found Jason in jail, Val felt there was hope. There was life in his eyes.

The sheriff shrugged. "I suppose I could go up now. I've got a deputy guarding the place from these damned reporters. Might be a good time to check on him and see what I can pick up."

Jason was surprised when Val brought over the rest of the pages without reading them first. He could tell she was curious about what Karen had written. And considering all she'd been through with him, he felt she deserved to know everything. After he read each page, he handed it through the bars to her.

He knew it was foolish to hope he would find something to prove him innocent. If Karen had known who rigged the gun in the safe, she never would have opened it herself. That was unless Val was right and Karen had wanted to get rid of him and had been rigging the gun herself when it went off.

But that, he didn't believe.

He read page after page, finding nothing. There was a paragraph about the necklace he'd sent from London. He'd thought she'd loved it. She hadn't.

It was clear she was lonely and depressed. Reading her ramblings, he felt guilty. He should have insisted she come over. So what if she'd said she was too tired. So what if he'd been busy twenty hours a day. They would have had four hours together. No wonder she'd turned to someone else.

By the time he finished reading through the pages they had, he still didn't know who her lover had been. She'd mentioned three men, all of them friends of his.

Or at least, he'd thought they were friends. One, obviously, wasn't.

Bud had taken her to a couple of functions, Gunther Marx had stopped by and helped her with her car, and Steve Jeffersons had brought her some books to read. Innocent enough acts. Friendly.

Handing the last page to Val, he sighed in frustration. Unless the sheriff came back with something more definitive, it looked as though he still wouldn't know.

Sheriff Maxwell returned thirty minutes later with the pages in a plastic bag. After clearing his desk, he carefully laid out the sodden sheets. Some were matted together. Others were so wet, they were about to disintegrate. Jason could see that handling them would be disastrous.

What he didn't expect was for the sheriff to come over and unlock his cell. "I presume you're not going to escape," he said, opening the door.

Jason chuckled and stepped out. "I love these small towns."

Where else but in Slaterville would an arresting officer set his prisoner free to read a diary? Or help peel pages apart? They all read what they could. In some places the ink had blurred; in others part of the page was missing. Days were out of order, destroying continuity, but Jason finally understood Karen's frame of mind the months before she died.

She was lonely, vulnerable.

And one of his friends had played on her loneliness, had been there the night she was questioning her attractiveness and femininity. If what she'd written was to be believed, she'd told Jason the truth. Only once was she unfaithful, and she'd regretted it.

She'd refused to tell him the name of the man, and her diary wasn't giving away her secret. The one page that had held the answer was so mutilated, only one line was legible. *I can't believe how jealous he is of Jason or that I actually slept with him.*

"Do you know who it was?" Val asked, touching his arm.

Jason glanced down at her hand, then at her face. No matter how hard he tried, he couldn't block her out. She wouldn't let him. "It could be any one of the three," he admitted, then leaned close and kissed her forehead. "I'm glad I understand, but none of this helps." He glanced at the sheriff. "In fact, it probably makes me look even more guilty."

"Irate husband kills wife in a fit of rage," the sheriff said. "It's happened thousands of times."

"Only this wasn't in a fit of rage," Val pointed out. "Jason's wife's murder was well planned."

"By someone who knew the combination to the wall safe." Jason remembered how the prosecuting attorney had harped on that point.

"Maybe your wife gave it to him. If not, why didn't this lover step forward during your trial?" Val asked. "Identify himself? That would have brought in a guilty verdict fast enough."

"Because he's my friend?" The word had an ironic twist.

"No, because he killed her."

"And why would he kill her?"

Val wished she had an answer to that. "I don't know."

Which put them back to square one. The diary had proved to be of no help. Sadly she watched Jason go back to his cell and the sheriff lock the door. "Don't give up hope, Jason," she pleaded. "I know you didn't do it."

He brushed his fingertips over her cheek, his gaze devouring her. "I love you," he whispered, then sighed and turned and walked away.

She took the diary pages home with her, along with Jason's other few possessions. Late into the night she reread every page, hoping she'd find something they'd missed the first time. It was after midnight when she went to bed, her eyes blurred and her head aching. If the answer was in the diary, she hadn't found it.

A crack of lightning woke her, bringing her to a sitting position. Seconds later thunder rumbled.

Her body trembling, she glanced at the clock. It was three A.M. Too early to be awake, but how could she sleep? Houses could explode. She knew that. Explode in the night.

In the night. The words echoed through her head. Lying back on her pillow, she listened to the storm and wondered why she had a nagging feeling she'd forgotten something.

And then she remembered.

At seven-thirty the next morning, Val stepped into the sheriff's office, walked by the deputy on duty, and stopped at Jason's cell. "I know who killed Karen. And that gun wasn't meant for her, no more than that explosion was meant for me. You're the one he's trying to kill."

FOURTEEN

Val sat staring at the tape recorder on the table. She knew it was ridiculous for a grown woman to get butterflies at the thought of reading one little speech onto a tape, but all she could remember was the time she'd brought home the speech she'd recorded in English class. She'd wanted to be on the debate team, but she'd needed her parents' okay. Her mother had said she sounded great, but her father had laughed at the idea and said no one with a voice like hers should talk into a tape recorder. The debate team was forgotten, and ever since, she'd avoiding talking into tape recorders. She'd even had Ginger record the message for her answering machine.

But Jason had said she'd be perfect.

Her finger shaking, she pressed the record button and began reading from the printed script. "Eldon Clifford died from a gunshot wound. He stumbled forward and fell dead right where you're standing, folks. But—"

Val snapped off the recorder and took a deep breath. Her hand was trembling so much, she could hardly read the words on the page, and if her voice sounded as shaky on the tape as it did to her ears, her father was right. She should not talk into a tape recorder.

It was Jason who was wrong. She wasn't the perfect voice for the lady-in-mourning. She wasn't even close.

Rewinding the tape, she played it back. No doubt about it. She sounded like Minnie Mouse. Her voice was too high. She was rushing the words. Everything was wrong.

Tape recorder in hand, she started up the stairs to the second floor, where Jason was working on the disappearing ghost. Once he heard how she actually sounded, he would agree. Debbie would be better. Or Julia.

She'd reached the top step when she heard the front door open. The other workers had left half an hour ago. Either someone had forgotten something and come back, or it was another one of those reporters who refused to give up. And if it was, she didn't envy him. At this hour of the night Jason wasn't too patient, especially with a media that wouldn't let him be.

Before she had a chance to step back down and look, a man called out. "Jason?"

She recognized the voice immediately. Bud Henke was here, in Slaterville. In the haunted house.

Only he shouldn't be.

Over a week had passed since she'd made the connection between Bud's call to her and the bomb going off at Jason's. Seven days since the sheriff had released Jason and the warrant had been issued for Bud's arrest. He should be in jail.

Barroom music began playing below, and she knew Bud had triggered the sensor for the first room. Another step or two and she would be able to see him.

Looking down, she watched the top of Bud's head come into view. His blond hair was tousled, and she was surprised by how small he looked. How innocent.

She knew better.

He had known the bomb had gone off at night, but she hadn't told him. He also worked at the studio where the police had traced the sale of the explosive. From that point on, it had been easy for them to prove Bud had been in Northern California the same time the bomb was planted. Credit cards told a lot.

There'd been enough evidence against Bud for Sheriff Maxwell to release Jason. Enough evidence to issue an arrest warrant for Bud.

Something clattered to the floor in the room behind Val, and Bud looked up, his gaze locking with hers. Her heart lurched to her throat, every muscle freezing in place.

"Jason up there?" Bud asked calmly, smiling his boyish smile and taking another step forward.

Val couldn't form the words to answer.

Jason picked up the screwdriver he'd dropped and slipped it into his tool belt. If that damned ghost didn't work this time, he didn't know what he'd do.

Stepping back out into the upstairs hallway, he started for the spot where the pressure sensor would trigger the hologram. Val stood at the top of the stairs, staring down them. From below he heard his own voice, the spiel so familiar, he was sick of it. He'd be glad when the old miner's hologram arrived, along with the actor's tape.

In a moment, he knew, there would be a gunshot.

It happened.

Then came a second shot.

"What the—?"

Wide-eyed, Val turned toward him, the color gone from her face. Just a whimper escaped her lips.

Jason took a step toward her, confused, only to run into her as she raced toward him. He nearly knocked the tape recorder from her hand. "Bu-ud," she stammered.

Only when he looked down the stairs did he realize what she'd said, and he immediately understood her fear. At the bottom of the stairs stood Bud, a pistol in his hand. His expression transfixed, he slowly raised his arm and aimed the gun their way.

Jason grabbed Val's arm and dragged her back with him. A shot went zinging over their heads. Too close, as far as Jason was concerned. He headed for the nearest bedroom.

"You won't get away this time," Bud yelled, coming up the stairs.

"How'd he get here?" Jason asked, knowing it wasn't a question Val could answer.

"Why isn't he in jail?" she asked back.

The moment they entered the bedroom, they triggered the corpse in the coffin. The ashen-faced mannequin slowly rose to a sitting position, his laughter filling the room. Jason cursed himself for activating the sensor. Bud would know which way they'd gone. No matter where they ran, they would set off a trail. They had to get out, but the emergency exit they planned on putting in hadn't been cut through the wall yet, the windows were all boarded up, and Bud was blocking the stairway. There was only one other alternative.

"Head for the passageway," Jason ordered, keeping

himself between Bud and Val. If they could get down the stone stairs and out the downstairs closet before Bud realized what they were doing, they had a chance, but they had to move fast.

Val slipped through the doorway before it swung completely open, and Jason quickly followed, pushing the door closed again. The lights along the base of the wall were positioned to give a clear view of each step. Val started down, still clutching the tape recorder, then paused and glanced back. "Keep going," he said, waving her on. "Get out and go for help."

"I'm not leaving without you."

"I'm right behind you."

A thump on the wall above them, then the creaking of springs as the door swung open, startled Jason. "How . . . ?" he muttered, then realized how Bud had found the panel. He'd told him where he could find it.

Jason remembered sitting in a bar with Bud his last trip to L.A., drinking a beer and telling him how he'd found a door that led to a secret passageway. He'd described where each door was located and how to find each latch. He should have kept his mouth shut.

Urging Val on, Jason followed close behind. Escaping through the downstairs closet was now an impossibility. Time was too limited. They had to make a run for the shed.

Jason had just reached the last step when a shot rang out. The sound was deafening in the enclosed area, the bullet pinging as it ricocheted off the slate rocks around them. Not stopping to think, he tackled Val, bringing her down to the ground. He didn't need her killed by a wild bullet.

"We're sitting ducks," he whispered in her ear. "We've got to kill the lights."

He pulled a utility knife from his tool belt and leaned closer to the wall. Grabbing the wire the electrician had strung along the base, he made his cut. Instantly the lights along the passageway went out.

Another shot was fired, the bullet again ricocheting from one rock to another. How many shots had that been? Jason wondered. Four? Five? He'd lost track. And did Bud have one clip or two?

As quietly as he could, Jason rose to his feet and helped Val up. They had the advantage. They knew the passageway, knew where every cobweb and bat had been placed. It would take Bud longer to negotiate the distance.

At least, Jason hoped it would.

"You're worse than a cat," Bud yelled into the darkness, sounding nearer than Jason wanted the man. "But lights or no lights, you're not lucking out, not like you've done all those other times."

Jason kept Val ahead of him as they moved along the passageway toward the shed. If Bud shot again, a caroming bullet could be as dangerous as leaving the lights on. He didn't want Val hit. If any shooting was going to take place, he wanted Bud to know where to aim.

"What other times?" Jason asked.

"You know," Bud said defiantly. "It would have been easy if I could have done this in the first place, but Bud wouldn't let me. He's always been such a wimp."

Ahead of him Jason heard a click and a soft whirring sound. He tensed, ready for an attack from that direction, then realized Val had started the tape recorder.

She spoke up, only a slight tremor in her voice hinting at her fear. "If Bud's a wimp, how does he stop you?"

The voice behind them immediately responded. "He won't let me out. Ever since I first helped him, he's acted like it was wrong. He got all upset when I set fire to our house. He was afraid the old man would take it out on him. But I knew *he* wasn't going to hurt anyone. *He* was through hurting us."

"He?" Val asked.

Jason could understand her confusion. He was confused.

"You know," came the answer. "*Him.* The old man. Bud called him Dad, but I never would. I hated him, and I had to kill him. Maybe Bud and the others were willing to live with what was happening, but I couldn't take it anymore."

"There are others?" Jason asked. He couldn't remember Bud ever saying anything about brothers or sisters.

"Oh, yes," Bud said casually. "They're not as strong as I am, and Bud won't let them out except at night when he's alone. Mostly they just want to play."

"But you're different," Val said. "Right?"

"I have to take care of him. Help him."

The idea was bizarre, but Jason was beginning to believe that the voice behind him, coming nearer and nearer, even as they hurried along through the dark passage, wasn't really Bud's. "And how will killing me help Bud?" he asked.

"He'll be the best then. He'll win the Oscars. Get the good movies. I knew the first time we met you that Bud would never succeed with you around. He wouldn't believe me then, said he needed you. But I knew what would happen. He actually thought he was going to be picked over you for the job with Spielberg. It wasn't until he lost out that he listened to me, let me out. But you and your nine lives. You lucked out, and your brother took the car that night."

Jason sucked in a breath and stopped walking. Val could tell and reached back, touching his arm. Every muscle in his body was tense. "You're saying you killed my brother?" Jason asked slowly.

"It was supposed to be you. I thought I did everything right. I knew a little air in the master cylinder would take the brake fluid out. How was I to know you'd let someone else drive your car? That I'd screwed up really upset Bud. He wouldn't let me come out after that, not until you got *Raptors.*"

"*Raptors,*" Jason repeated, and Val could feel the muscles in his arm tense even more. She urged him to move on.

"That should have been Bud's picture. His ideas were better than yours." The voice in the darkness laughed. "I knew he was upset when he didn't object to our flying to England to pay you a visit. You know, you really should have been under that prop when it fell. You had been, just the minute before."

"I had a call," Jason said quietly, and Val knew he was remembering. She'd also noticed that Bud sounded closer. Holding on to Jason's hand, she tried to move faster. They had enough on tape. They needed to get out.

"And then when you came back from England," Bud went on.

An icy chill passed over Val. She wasn't sure if they'd reached that spot near the shed where it was always a little cooler, of it if was the realization of just how sick Bud was and what he was going to say next.

"What about when I came back from England?" Jason asked cautiously.

Bud sighed. "Karen wasn't supposed to open that safe. She'd told me she never did. Remember when you called from England and asked her to get some papers from the safe and mail them to you? I was there with her. I watched her open the safe. She had to try the combination twice before she remembered. She laughed when she told me how she always mixed up the numbers, dialing 5294 instead of 5924."

"You rigged the gun," Jason said, understanding. Everything was fitting into place.

"Of course," Bud said. "Actually it was very easy to do. Your wife had a headache. She was always getting headaches. So I was helpful, I got her a couple of aspirins, only they were sleeping pills, not aspirins. Once she was asleep, I went to work. I had everything set up and all traces of what I'd done cleaned up by the time she woke. All I had to do was tell her we'd made love, and she didn't question why I was still there. In fact, she was so upset about that, she didn't think of anything else."

"You never actually made love with her?"

Bud laughed. "I should have. It would have served you right. I guess I'll have to be satisfied with killing you and your new girlfriend."

Jason knew they had to get out of the passageway. He also knew the door to the shed should be only a few feet away. But they'd left the light on in the shed. There would be a moment when Val opened the door that she would be a perfect target. For that moment he had to distract Bud.

"Go!" he ordered, giving her a shove forward.

He heard a clunk and hoped it was the tape recorder hitting the wall and not her body. He waited for her to open the door.

"I'm not leaving without you," she said firmly.

No light pierced the darkness and he knew she understood his plan. Darn her and her stubbornness. "Get out of here," he said.

The gunshot vibrated through his ears, the hiss of the bullet too close. This one didn't ricochet. With a thud it buried itself in something solid.

"Val!" he cried, reaching out and groping for her in the darkness.

"I'm okay," she said, her bravery noticeably weakened.

"Get out so I can get out!"

"I—"

He didn't think she would do it, then a slash of light cut through the darkness. Though it might be the last time he saw her, Jason didn't watch her leave. Waving his arms and jumping around, he tried to distract Bud.

For just a second he saw his friend . . . saw the gun. Then another shot went off.

The media had a heyday with the story. Val had gotten everything on tape, and excerpts were played on all of the major newscasts. Once again Jason's picture appeared in the papers, along with Bud's, the rivalry between the two special effects experts fully dramatized. Bud's multiple personalities and death from a ricocheting bullet in a secret passageway of a haunted house gave the story the ironic twist it needed.

Val knew they couldn't have bought better publicity. The only problem was finding time to work on the house so they could get it open to take advantage of that publicity.

They set the thirtieth of September as the opening day. It would be a special occasion, and a select few would be their honored guests. Others would be given the opportunity to pay one hundred dollars each to join the tour, all proceeds to go to WIN and the safe house. The governor of California would be there, along with several members of Congress, the mayor of Slaterville, Hollywood celebrities, and a few members of the press. Val knew that for Jason the two most important guests that night would be his parents. They arrived the day before.

"I think you were wrong about your parents," she said to Jason the morning of the thirtieth, stretching as she sat up in bed and watched him come into the bedroom with two steaming mugs of coffee.

"How's that?" he asked, setting one mug on the night table by her side.

She watched him walk around the bed, the sweatpants he'd slipped on to go make the coffee low on his hips. Nothing covered his top half except for the dark hairs she loved twisting around her fingers after they'd made love. He set his mug on his night table, then slid back under the sheet.

She waited until he was beside her before answering. "Maybe your parents will always hold your brother up as the model child, but you can tell from the way they talk about all the trouble you got into as a child that they're proud of your, ah . . . flair."

Jason's chuckle came from deep within his chest. "I don't think either of them would call it flair. In fact, I think the words my father used last night were 'bothersome' and 'mischievous.'"

Val knew the words didn't matter. It was the tears that had been in his mother's eyes when she first embraced him, and the choked-up way his father had gotten. And the way they'd talked about Jason to her. It would still take a while, but the wound was healing.

"You were mischievous when you said you weren't going back to L.A. When are you going to tell them about that movie you just agreed to do?"

"When everything's firmed up." He turned to her, his dark brows forming a heavy line over even darker eyes. "Do you want me to go back to L.A.?"

No, she wanted to cry out. Instead, she forced herself to be reasonable. "You have to. You don't need to hide anymore. Slaterville's not the place for you."

"No, it's not," he agreed too readily. "I doubt the information highway will make its way through here for a while."

"And there's not too many haunted houses to fix up." Biting her lower lip, she picked up her mug. She didn't want to talk about his leaving. She didn't even want to think about it.

He ran a fingertip up the side of her neck, just behind her ear, and a shiver of excitement raced down her spine. How well he'd learned where to touch her to get an immediate response. How desolate she was going to be when he left.

"Don't," she said, pulling away.

"Don't what?" he asked, dropping his finger to her arm, just below the sleeve of the nightshirt she'd slipped on after he'd said he would make coffee. From there he burned a sensitive trail to her wrist.

"Don't do that." She pulled her arm away and put the mug back on the table. "I'm not in the mood."

"Mood for what?" he asked innocently, letting his hand and his gaze stray down to where the sheet covered her hips.

She pressed her hands on either side of her legs, keeping the sheet snug over them. "You know what. We've got a lot to do today. You said it yourself. It's going to be hell, talking to the media . . . entertaining the bigwigs."

"You haven't answered my question," he said softly, back to running his fingertip up the side of her neck.

Again a shiver traveled down her spine. "Which was?"

"Do *you* want me to go to L.A.?"

She looked away. "If you don't go, you won't be happy."

"And if I do go, will you be happy?"

She knew the answer to that. Just thinking of him leaving was tearing her apart inside. But her feelings didn't matter. She knew what happened when you tried to hang on to something that wouldn't work. People got hurt.

Her gaze was clear when she looked at him. "You can't depend on finding your happiness in others. You have to find it in yourself."

Jason shook his head and scowled. "You're avoiding the question."

Moving quickly, he dislodged her hands from their

protective positions by her sides and slid his body over hers so that his face was only inches above hers. His arms held his weight off her chest, and his knees spanned hers. His sweatpants rubbed against her bare legs, and through her nightshirt she could feel her breasts touching his chest. Her nipples grew hard, and she sucked in a breath. "Jason?"

"Do you love me?"

She'd told him she did at least a thousand times. There was no way she could deny it now. "Yes."

"Yet you want me to leave?"

"You have to."

"Because of my career?"

"Yes."

"Okay, let's approach this from a different angle." He leaned close and kissed the side of her mouth. A taste of coffee lingered on his lips, telling her he'd had a sip before bringing hers into the bedroom. When he lifted his head, she knew that from any angle she loved him.

"Do you like living in Slaterville?" he asked, looking down at her.

Her answer was easy. "Yes."

"If you couldn't live here, where would you want to live?" He pulled back slightly, gazing into her eyes. His hips touched hers, and she could feel he wasn't aroused. Her answer, at the moment, was more important than sex.

The place, she realized, didn't matter, but her answer would make her vulnerable. Though he'd told her he loved her, that had been before they'd found out about Bud. Since then he had never said the words, and the subject of marriage had never come up. Unsure what his reaction would be, she said what was in her heart. "Anywhere with you."

His smile came slowly; the breath he released was long and deep. "I don't want to go back to L.A., but I can't do what needs to be done from here. Dennis Muren and ILM are doing fine in Northern California, proving a special effects workshop doesn't need to be in Hollywood. All I need is to find a place near a major airport, in a location where it's easy to hook up with today's technology. The money I'll be getting now that the question of Karen's death has been resolved, should help us find something suitable."

"Or we could always create a haunted house to bring in extra money," she joked.

"In your dreams." Once again he leaned close. "So?"

"So, what?" She thought she'd answered his question.

"Will you marry me?"

It was her turn to smile. "Is that a proposal?"

"As close as you'll probably get. What do you say?"

"What about Karen?"

Again a frown furrowed his brow. "What about her?"

Val sighed. "How can you marry me when you're still in love with her?"

"Is that what you think? That I'm still in love with Karen?"

She looked into his eyes and nodded.

"Oh, sweet Valerie." A smile softened his craggy features, and his voice was a warm caress. "I'm not going to tell you I didn't love her or that I'll forget the years we had together, but what I feel for you is different. You came into my life when I was at my lowest ebb; you gave me your trust and brought me hope. How could I still love Karen when I love you so much, when you're the woman I want to spend the rest of my life with?"

She let his words chase away her fears and knew she would never again be jealous of the life he'd lived before they met. It was the life they had ahead of them that needed their attention. Slowly she grinned. "If you're spending the rest of your life with me, I guess we'd better get married."

His mouth covered hers, this kiss different from the one before. Fuller. Deeper. More intense in the sensations it created and more satisfying. And when he once again pulled back, she felt the change it had produced lower in his body.

There were no "don'ts" when he trailed kisses along the side of her neck, no "don'ts" when he slipped off his sweatpants and pulled off her nightshirt. She wanted him doing those special things with his hands that created effects in her she would never grow tired of. She wanted the fantasy to go on, forever and ever.

THE EDITOR'S CORNER

Prepare to be swept off your feet by the four sizzling LOVESWEPT romances available next month. Never mind puppy love—you're soon to experience the tumultuous effects of desperation and passion in this spring's roller-coaster of romance.

Bestselling author Fayrene Preston turns up the heat with **LADY BEWARE**, LOVE-SWEPT #742. Kendall Merrick trusts Steven Gant when she should be running for her life. From the moment they meet, she is certain she knows him—knows his warmth, his scent, and the heat of his caress—but it just isn't possible! Steven hints she is in danger, then tempts her with fiery kisses that make her forget any fear. Has she surrendered to a stranger who will steal her soul? Find out in this spellbinding tale from Fayrene Preston.

Change gears with Marcia Evanick's playful but passionate **EMMA AND THE HAND-SOME DEVIL**, LOVESWEPT #743. She figures Brent Haywood will be happy to sell his half of Amazing Grace, but when the gorgeous hunk says he is staying, Emma Carson wonders what he could possibly want with a chicken farm—or her! Fascinated by his spunky housemate, Brent senses her yearnings, guesses at the silk she wears beneath the denim, and hopes that his lips can silence her fear of never being enough for him. Discover if opposites really do attract as Marcia Evanick explores the humor and touching emotion of unexpected love.

THICK AS THIEVES, LOVESWEPT #744, is Janis Reams Hudson's latest steamy suspense. Undercover agent Harper Montgomery stands alone as his brother is buried, remembering how Mike had stolen his future and married the woman who should have been *his* wife. Now, ten years later, Annie is no longer the carefree woman he remembers. Harper is determined to learn the bitter truth behind the sadness and fear in her eyes—and find out whether there is anything left of the old Annie, the one who had sworn their love was forever. Janis Reams Hudson fans the flames of reawakened love in this sizzling contemporary romance.

Join us in welcoming new author Riley Morse as we feature her sparkling debut, **INTO THE STORM**, LOVESWEPT #745. If all is fair in love and war, Dr. Ryan Jericho declares the battle lines drawn! Summer Keaton's golden beauty is true temptation, but the software she has designed will cost him a halfway house for kids he counsels—unless he distracts her long enough to break the deal. Scorched by a gaze that lights a fire of longing, Summer struggles to survive his seduction strategy without losing her heart. Riley Morse creates a pair of tantalizing adversaries in this fabulous love story.

Happy reading,

With warmest wishes!

Beth de Guzman

Shauna Summers

Beth de Guzman   Shauna Summers
Senior Editor   Associate Editor

P.S. Don't miss the exciting women's fiction Bantam has coming in June: In **FAIREST OF THEM ALL**, Teresa Medeiros's blockbuster medieval romance, Sir Austyn of Gavenmore, in search of a plain bride, wins Holly de Chastel in a tournament, never suspecting her to be the fairest woman in all of England; Geralyn Dawson's enticing new charmer, **TEMPTING MO-RALITY**, has Zach Burnett conceiving a plan to use Morality Brown for his personal revenge—only to have the miracle of love save his soul. Look for a sneak peek at these dazzling books in next month's LOVESWEPT. And immediately following this page, look for a preview of the terrific romances from Bantam that are *available now!*

Don't miss these extraordinary books
by your favorite Bantam authors

On sale in April:

DARK RIDER
by Iris Johansen

LOVE STORM
by Susan Johnson

PROMISE ME MAGIC
by Patricia Camden

"Iris Johansen is one of the romance genre's finest treasures."
—*Romantic Times*

DARK RIDER
by the *New York Times* bestselling author
IRIS JOHANSEN

New York Times *bestselling author Iris Johansen is a "master among master storytellers"* and her bestselling novels have won every major romance award, including the* coveted Romantic Times *Lifetime Achievement Award. Now discover the spellbinding world of Iris Johansen in her most tantalizing novel yet.*

From the moment she heard of the arrival of the English ship, Cassandra Deville sensed danger. But she never expected the sensuous invader who stepped out of the shadows of the palms and onto the moonlit beach. Bold, passionate, electrifyingly masculine, Jared Danemount made it clear he had every intention of destroying her father. But he hardly knew what to make of the exquisite, pagan creature who offered herself to him, defiantly declaring that she

* Affaire de Coeur

*would use his desire to her own advantage. Still, he could
no more resist her challenge than he could ignore the temptation to risk everything for the heart of a woman sworn to
betray him.*

"Are you truly a virgin?"

She stiffened and then whirled to face the man
strolling out of the thatch of palms. He spoke in the
Polynesian language she had used with her friends,
but there could be no doubt that he was not one of
them. He was as tall but leaner and moved with a
slow, casual grace, not with the springy exuberance of
the islanders. He was dressed in elegant tight
breeches and his coat fit sleekly over his broad shoulders. His snowy cravat was tied in a complicated fall
and his dark hair bound back in a queue.

*He is very beautiful and has the grace and lusty appe-
tite of that stallion you love so much.*

Her friend Lihua had said those words and she
was right. He *was* beautiful. Exotic grace and strength
exuded from every limb. High cheekbones and that
well-formed, sensual mouth gave his face a fascinating
quality that made it hard to tear her gaze away. A
stray breeze ruffled his dark hair and a lock fell across
his wide forehead.

Pagan.

The word came out of nowhere and she instantly
dismissed it. Their housekeeper Clara used the term
to describe the islanders and she would deem it totally
unfit for civilized young noblemen. Yet there
was something free and reckless flickering in the
stranger's expression that she had never seen in any of
the islanders.

Yes, he must be the Englishman; he was coming from the direction of King Kamehameha's village, she realized. He probably only wanted supplies or trade rights as the other English did. She did not have to worry about him.

"Well, are you?" he asked lazily as he continued to walk toward her.

He might not be a threat but she answered with instinctive wariness. "You should not eavesdrop on others' conversations. It's not honorable."

"I could hardly keep from hearing. You were shouting." His gaze wandered from her face to her bare breasts and down to her hips swathed in the cotton sarong. "And I found the subject matter so very intriguing. It was exceptionally . . . arousing. It's not every day a man is compared to a stallion."

His arrogance and confidence were annoying. "Lihua is easily pleased."

He looked startled, but then a slow smile lit his face. "And you are not, if you're still a virgin. What a challenge to a man. What is your name?"

"What is yours?"

"Jared."

"You have another name."

His brows lifted. "You're not being fair. You've not told me your name yet." He bowed. "But, if we must be formal, I'm Jared Barton Danemount."

"And you're a duke?"

"I have that honor . . . or dishonor. Depending upon my current state of dissipation. Does that impress you?"

"No, it's only another word for chief, and we have many chiefs here."

He laughed. "I'm crushed. Now that we've established my relative unimportance, may I ask your name?"

"Kanoa." It was not a lie. It was the Polynesian name she had been given, and meant more to her than her birth name.

"The free one," the Englishman translated. "But you're not free. Not if this person you called the ugly one keeps you from pleasure."

"That's none of your concern."

"On the contrary, I hope to make it very much my concern. I've had very good news tonight and I feel like celebrating. Will you celebrate with me, Kanoa?"

His smile shimmered in the darkness, coaxing, alluring. Nonsense. He was only a man; it was stupid to be so fascinated by this stranger. "Why should I? Your good news is nothing to me."

"Because it's a fine night and I'm a man and you're a woman. Isn't that enough?"

LOVE STORM
by Susan Johnson

"Susan Johnson is one of the best."
—*Romantic Times*

Desperate to avoid a loathsome match, Zena Turku ran from the glittering ballroom in the snowy night and threw herself at the mercy of a darkly handsome stranger. He was her only hope of escape, her one guarantee of safe passage to her ancestral home in the Caucasus mountains. But Prince Alexander Kuzan mistook the alluring redhead for a lady of the evening, the perfect plaything to relieve the boredom of his country journey. Only after her exquisite innocence was revealed did the most notorious rake of St. Petersburg realize that his delicious game of seduction had turned into a conquest of his heart.

Zena experienced a frightening feeling of vulnerability when this darkly handsome prince touched her; it was as though she no longer belonged to herself, as though he controlled her passion with his merest touch.

The prince must think her the most degraded wanton to allow him such liberties, to actually beg for release in his arms. A deep sense of humiliation swept over her as she tried to reconcile this astonishing, unprecedented sensuousness with the acceptable behavior required of young society debutantes. How could she have permitted these rapturous feelings of hers to overcome her genteel upbringing? Certainly the prince would never respect her now.

Zena's eyelashes fluttered up and she gazed surreptitiously from under their shield at the man who had so casually taken her virginity. He was disturbingly handsome: fine, aristocratic features; full, sensitive mouth; dark, long, wavy hair; smooth bronze skin. The brilliance of a huge emerald caught her eye as his hand rested possessively on her hip, making her acutely aware of the contrast between their circumstances. He was handsome, rich, charming, seductively expert, she ruefully noted. Plainly she had made a fool of herself, and her mortification was absolute. But then she reminded herself sharply that *anything* was superior to having to wed that odious toad of a general, and the prince *was* taking her away from St. Petersburg.

The emerald twinkled in the subdued light as Alex gently brushed the damp curls from Zena's cheek. "I'm sorry for hurting you, *ma petite*," he whispered softly. "I had no idea this was your first evening as a streetwalker. Had I known, I could have been more gentle."

At which point Prince Alexander was presented with some fascinating information, most of which he would have quite willingly remained in ignorance of.

"I'm not a streetwalker, my lord."

Alex's black brows snapped together in a sudden scowl. *Bloody hell, what have I got into?*

"I'm the daughter of Baron Turku from Astrakhan."

The scowl deepened noticeably.

"My father died six months ago, and my aunt began trying to marry me off to General Scobloff."

The frown lifted instantly, and Alex breathed a sigh of relief. At least, he mentally noted, there were no irate relatives to reckon with immediately. "Sweet Jesus! That old vulture must be close to seventy!" he exclaimed, horrified.

"Sixty-one, my lord, and he's managed to bury two wives already," Zena quietly murmured. "I didn't want to become his wife, but my aunt was insisting, so I simply had to get away. My little brother and I will—"

"Little brother?" Alex sputtered. "The young child isn't yours?" he asked in confusion, and then remembered. Of course he wasn't hers; Alex had just taken her virginity! A distinct feeling of apprehension and, on the whole, disagreeable sensations struck the young prince. *Merde!* This just wasn't his night! "You deliberately led me on," he accused uncharitably, choosing to ignore the fact that he had drunk so much in the past fifteen hours that his clarity of thought was not at peak performance.

"I did not lead you on!" Zena returned tartly, angry that the prince should think she had contrived this entire situation. "Modest young ladies of good breeding do not lead men on!" she snapped.

"Permit me to disagree, my pet, for I've known many modest young ladies of good breeding," Alex disputed coolly, "a number of whom have led me on to the same, ah, satisfactory conclusion we have just enjoyed. They're all quite willing once the tiresome conventional posturing has been observed."

The prince's obvious competence in an area of

connoisseurship completely foreign to Zena's limited sphere served to squelch her ingenuous assertion.

Alex sighed disgruntledly. *Good God, for which of my sins am I paying penance?* "What am I to do with you—a damnable virgin? Of all the rotten luck! You try to be helpful and come to the aid of what appears to be a nice, ordinary streetwalker and look what happens. She turns out to be a cursed green virgin with a baby brother to boot, not to mention a respectable family."

"No, my lord, no family," Zena quietly reminded him.

A faintly pleased glint of relief momentarily shone in the depths of the golden eyes. "Thank God for small favors. Nevertheless, you, my dear, have become a vexatious problem," Alex censoriously intoned.

"You could take the honorable course of action and marry me, my lord."

PROMISE ME MAGIC

by the extraordinarily talented

Patricia Camden

"A strong new voice in historical fiction . . . This is an author to watch!"
—*Romantic Times*

With a fury born of fear, Katharina had taken aim at the bandit who dared to trespass on her land and fired only to discover that the powerful warrior she felled was a man she thought long dead . . . a man who had stolen her fortune . . . a man she despised. Now, as she gazed into Alexandre von Löwe's smoldering gray eyes and felt the overpowering pull of his attraction, she wondered why she'd let the scoundrel live and how she was going to tell him she was masquerading as his wife. . . .

"I am Katharina von Melle," she told him, then waited as if expecting a response.

"Madame von Melle," he said, giving her a slight nod. He grimaced and bit back a ripe oath. Someone had just lit the powder touchhole of the cannon in his head.

"Katharina," the woman gritted out as if to a slow wit. "Anna. Magdalena. von Melle."

Obviously, she thought he should know her. A

memory niggled, but it was beyond grasping in his fuzzy head. Christ, she was beautiful. Full lips hinting at a sensual nature that belied the coldness in her eyes, the bones—if not her manner or her clothes—telling of well-bred nobility.

A former lover? Had he passed the long months of a year's winter quarters spending his passion in that glorious voluptuous body? One forgot a great many things in war, some by accident, others for the sake of sanity, but, sweet God, he'd take her gun and shoot himself if he could ever have forgotten that body—or those eyes.

Katharina von Melle. It felt as if he should remember it, but . . . nothing. "Madame von Melle, of course!" he prevaricated. "The wounds of war have addled my wits. Such eyes as those would be forever burned into any man's memor—" The slender finger curling on the trigger tightened. "I mean, that is—"

" 'I mean, that is' . . . utter nonsense, Colonel von Löwe," she said, her gaze as steady as a cat's. "If there is any burning to be done, it will be into your body by a lead ball."

As a cat's . . . Katharina von Melle. *Oh, Jesus.* "Kat," he said. "You're Father's Kat." They had never met, but he knew her. God save him, he knew her.

"You blanch quite nicely," she told him. "I take it you recognize the name? Your *ward*, my dear Colonel. I was your ward. First your father's, then *yours*. Do you remember now? I was part of your inheritance, remember? Your eldest brother was to get the north end of this valley, complete with the lucrative mill, your middle brother was to get all the land in the middle, from the peak known as the Mule in the west to the Carabas River. And you—all you were to inherit was the small manor house of Löwe and a mangy spinster named Kat. And you did inherit. First the house and me, and then the rest of it when your brothers died, and all without bothering to leave your precious war."

He wanted to sleep and the careless irritation that comes from being deprived of it was gnawing at his sense of preservation. "Did you truly expect me to leave my regiment and come home to a ramshackle old house to nursemaid the bastard daughter of some friend of my father's I don't even know? The French had entered the war! Old alliances were falling apart; new alliances were being formed. It was as if a puddle of mercury had dispersed into a hundred bubbles, some that would save you, others that would prove fatal." He shrugged, but had to look away from the winter in her eyes. "An ink-stained lawyer's clerk sent word that you were living with friends in the Tausend capital. It seemed adequate to me. I had more important things to deal with—such as a war."

"War or no, alliances or no—you still managed to turn inheriting this Kat into a profit, didn't you? A ten-thousand thaler profit! My marriage portion. But I didn't know that then, did I? No. I discovered it six years ago when word came that you were dead. At last! At age twenty-two I found myself mistress of my fortune and my fate—except, of course, that there was no fortune. That loss cost me dearly, von Löwe. But though you cost me while alive, by being dead you have managed to partially pay me back. Löwe Manor is mine."

"Impossible."

"No, Colonel von Löwe, *possible*. In fact, more than possible. It has been done. A fait accompli. Löwe Manor is mine. For four years I have lived there, and no one has challenged me." A mixture of guilt and bravado flashed through her eyes, the same look a woman gets who has cheated on her lover and now seeks to deny it. He had barely registered that it was there before it was gone. She sighted again down the barrel of the pistol with renewed determination.

"And now, Colonel, though you neglected to give me a choice about my future when you stole my fortune from me, I shall give you a choice about yours. You can choose to leave—with Löwe remaining in my possession—or you can choose to contest my ownership. Of course, if you choose the latter, the hero dies, shot for a brigand on his way home. Such a shame."

"So the bastard daughter would turn murderer? Such a shame."

He heard her lick her lips. "You and Tragen and the other one can move to Alte Veste. It is but a day's ride from here."

"A day's ride straight up. It's coming on to winter, Kat . . . Katharina," he said carefully. "Alte Veste is deserted, and has been for three generations. Cold, too, and full of drafts. Tragen would probably succumb."

He waited, his breathing nearly suspended. He needed the obscurity that Löwe Manor could provide —at least until late February or early March. And after that, given von Mecklen's delight in all things ravaged, they all would most likely be looking for a new place to live. If they were still alive.

"You may stay until Tragen has recovered enough to travel. But you must give me your word that Löwe is mine."

He sucked in a breath of victory. "You have it."

"Say the words."

"I give you my word that Löwe Manor will be yours."

"Not will be . . . *is!*" She moved around to where Alexandre could see her, and what he saw made him go still inside. Distrust, despair, and an iron will to go on. It was the look of a woman touched too closely by war. He'd seen it before, on other women's faces, on those who had survived.

"Löwe is yours," he said softly.

"And . . . and you must accept whatever you find there."

He narrowed his eyes. "Why? What will I find there?" She did not answer. "What will I find there, Kat?" Silence. He let his head fall back to the folded wool, but through his lashes he could still see the black point of the pistol barrel aimed at him. "I will accept whatever I find there . . . within the restrictions of my oaths to the emperor, the duke of Tausend, and my men."

The gun barrel did not waver for a heartbeat. Then two . . . three . . .

"Cross me and you're a dead man," Katharina said with the tempered steel of conviction. And lowered the pistol.

He closed his eyes in relief. Whatever desperate hold he'd had on his awareness left him then, and he began to slip into sleep.

A nudge roused him to semiawareness. "Colonel

von Löwe," she called, nudging him again. "Colonel, there's one thing you should know before we reach Löwe Manor."

He grunted, drifting back into oblivion.

"I'm your wife."

Alexandre woke up.

And don't miss these electrifying
romances from Bantam Books,
on sale in May:

FAIREST OF THEM ALL
by bestselling author
Teresa Medeiros
"Teresa Medeiros writes rare love
stories to cherish."
—*Romantic Times*

TEMPTING MORALITY
by award-winning author
Geralyn Dawson
"[Geralyn Dawson] weaves a deliciously
arousing tale."
—*Affaire de Coeur*

To enter the sweepstakes outlined below, you must respond by the date specified and follow all entry instructions published elsewhere in this offer.

DREAM COME TRUE SWEEPSTAKES

Sweepstakes begins 9/1/94, ends 1/15/96. To qualify for the Early Bird Prize, entry must be received by the date specified elsewhere in this offer. Winners will be selected in random drawings on 2/29/96 by an independent judging organization whose decisions are final. Early Bird winner will be selected in a separate drawing from among all qualifying entries.

Odds of winning determined by total number of entries received. Distribution not to exceed 300 million.

Estimated maximum retail value of prizes: Grand (1) $25,000 (cash alternative $20,000); First (1) $2,000; Second (1) $750; Third (50) $75; Fourth (1,000) $50; Early Bird (1) $5,000. Total prize value: $86,500.

Automobile and travel trailer must be picked up at a local dealer; all other merchandise prizes will be shipped to winners. Awarding of any prize to a minor will require written permission of parent/guardian. If a trip prize is won by a minor, s/he must be accompanied by parent/legal guardian. Trip prizes subject to availability and must be completed within 12 months of date awarded. Blackout dates may apply. Early Bird trip is on a space available basis and does not include port charges, gratuities, optional shore excursions and onboard personal purchases. Prizes are not transferable or redeemable for cash except as specified. No substitution for prizes except as necessary due to unavailability. Travel trailer and/or automobile license and registration fees are winners' responsibility as are any other incidental expenses not specified herein.

Early Bird Prize may not be offered in some presentations of this sweepstakes. Grand through third prize winners will have the option of selecting any prize offered at level won. All prizes will be awarded. Drawing will be held at 204 Center Square Road, Bridgeport, NJ 08014. Winners need not be present. For winners list (available in June, 1996), send a self-addressed, stamped envelope by 1/15/96 to: Dream Come True Winners, P.O. Box 572, Gibbstown, NJ 08027.

THE FOLLOWING APPLIES TO THE SWEEPSTAKES ABOVE:

No purchase necessary. No photocopied or mechanically reproduced entries will be accepted. Not responsible for lost, late, misdirected, damaged, incomplete, illegible, or postage-die mail. Entries become the property of sponsors and will not be returned.

Winner(s) will be notified by mail. Winner(s) may be required to sign and return an affidavit of eligibility/release within 14 days of date on notification or an alternate may be selected. Except where prohibited by law, entry constitutes permission to use of winners' names, hometowns, and likenesses for publicity without additional compensation. Void where prohibited or restricted. All federal, state, provincial, and local laws and regulations apply.

All prize values are in U.S. currency. Presentation of prizes may vary; values at a given prize level will be approximately the same. All taxes are winners' responsibility.

Canadian residents, in order to win, must first correctly answer a time-limited skill testing question administered by mail. Any litigation regarding the conduct and awarding of a prize in this publicity contest by a resident of the province of Quebec may be submitted to the Regie des loteries et courses du Quebec.

Sweepstakes is open to legal residents of the U.S., Canada, and Europe (in those areas where made available) who have received this offer.

Sweepstakes in sponsored by Ventura Associates, 1211 Avenue of the Americas, New York, NY 10036 and presented by independent businesses. Employees of these, their advertising agencies and promotional companies involved in this promotion, and their immediate families, agents, successors, and assignees shall be ineligible to participate in the promotion and shall not be eligible for any prizes covered herein.   SWP 3/95